The Voice

The Voice
and other stories

SEICHO MATSUMOTO

Translated by Adam Kabat

KODANSHA INTERNATIONAL
Tokyo and New York

The stories included in this volume were first published in Japanese under the following titles: *Kyōhansha*, 1965 (The Accomplice); *Kao*, 1959 (The Face); *Chihō-shi o kau onna*, 1959 (The Serial); *Sōsa kengai no jōken*, 1959 (Beyond All Suspicion); *Koe*, 1959 (The Voice); *Kantō-ku no onna*, 1960 (The Woman Who Wrote Haiku).

Distributed in the United States by Kodansha International/ USA Ltd., 114 Fifth Avenue, New York, New York 10011. Published by Kodansha International Ltd., 2-2 Otowa 1-chome, Bunkyo-ku, Tokyo 112 and Kodansha International/USA Ltd., 114 Fifth Avenue, New York, New York 10011.
First edition, 1989

Library of Congress Cataloging-in-Publication Data

Matsumoto, Seichō, 1909–
    The Voice and other stories.

    1. Matsumoto, Seichō, 1909–   —Translations,
English. I. Title.
PL856.A8A25   1989   895.6'35   88-81846
ISBN 0-87011-895-1 (U.A.)
ISBN 4-7700-1395-7 (Japan)

Contents

The Accomplice

1

Hikosuke Uchibori believed himself to be a success. His store, which sold furniture on credit, was well known throughout Fukuoka City. Advertised as a "furniture department store," in five years his business had grown remarkably and now had a firmly established reputation, much to the amazement of the longstanding businessmen in the area.

Hikosuke's success may have been due to the skills he had acquired during his long years as a traveling salesman, although then he hadn't been selling furniture. For fifteen years he had peddled dinnerware, making the rounds of department stores and wholesalers throughout the country. The dealer he worked for had exclusive distribution rights for a well-known brand of dinnerware that was even exported to as far away as India.

Hikosuke would pass through the doors of wholesalers in every region, carrying a suitcase full of neatly arranged samples. He'd show his samples and take their orders, and he'd be given a check for any outstanding accounts. With his busy schedule, he had no time to waste before heading off to his next client. Forever consulting train timetables, that was the life he had led for fifteen years.

"Traveling around Japan all year long must take you to lots of interesting places," people had often said to him.

Hikosuke had found such ignorance irksome. He was doing his job; he wasn't on a pleasure jaunt. From the station he'd go directly to his client. Then after visiting two or three stores, he'd head back to the station and rush on to his next stop, for he had a tight schedule to keep. Even in the train he'd be filling out order slips and checking the accounts of each store, which left him little time to gaze at the scenery. When his work was over, he might stare absently out the window, but even then his head would be filled with all sorts of worries—lack of orders, outstanding accounts, bouncing checks, customer complaints, and so on—making him oblivious to the scenery.

At night he would economize by staying at the cheapest inns. If he happened to be at a famous tourist spot or hot spring resort, he'd always feel despondent. The sight of tourists having a good time would bring home the wretchedness of his own situation. They may have been fellow travelers, but they were a world apart. He'd compare himself, in his dusty clothes and carrying an aluminum suitcase, with a passerby sporting a fancy new suit, a camera dangling from one shoulder and a beautiful woman on his arm. When he lay down on his thin mattress, there were nights he couldn't sleep out of envy for some such stranger.

That was Hikosuke's life up until five years ago. Now he was worth nearly ten million yen. Even if this figure included the merchandise in his store and his accounts receivable, it was still enormous. He had reached a position in life where he could indulge in any luxury he pleased, and he looked back on his former self with nothing but pity.

However, there was more to Hikosuke's past than memories of hard-up bygone days, for it held a dark and threatening secret. Recently, this would suddenly spring out and catch him unawares.

Hikosuke's success was built on his business acumen, but his initial capital had originated from somewhere else. No traveling salesman could hope to earn that kind of money: his fifteen years of poverty were sufficient proof of this.

The truth was that Hikosuke had robbed a bank to get the money, and in the process someone had been killed. The incident had occurred in an old castle town by the side of a lake in the Sanin area. He had broken into the local bank, whose old-fashioned architecture perfectly matched the town, and made off with five million yen.

However, he hadn't used all the money for capital. Half of it he had given to his partner as they had agreed beforehand. It was his partner who had insisted that they split it fifty-fifty.

Something like robbing a bank could never be achieved alone. A second person was necessary to egg one on. There's no need here to go into the reasons in detail, but a bank robbery is the type of job where you need a partner.

Hikosuke's accomplice was Takeji Machida, who was thirty-five or six, about eight years younger than Hikosuke. Takeji had a long, weasely face, a pale complexion, and a cheerless disposition. Even now, Hikosuke could recall, with a shudder of distaste, the washed-out, beady eyes and the thin, unsmiling lips.

Takeji was also a traveling salesman who carried a suitcase stuffed with samples. However, he dealt in lacquerware. The two men got acquainted because they often ran into each other at the same store.

2

It was Takeji who first came up with the idea. In that sense, he could be considered the main culprit.

The two traveling salesmen, with no prospects for the future, hatched their scheme in a cramped hotel room they shared. But it was Hikosuke who led the actual robbery. He had often used this small bank to transfer money every month, so he was familiar with the layout.

The bank manager lived on the premises in the rear of the building, and their plan hinged on this piece of information. Around 8:00 P.M. the employees working overtime turned off the lights and went home. The two broke in soon after.

When they brandished knives in the manager's face, he took

out his keys and opened the doors of the vault. But once they had stuffed two bags full of money, the manager started to make a fuss, and Takeji stabbed him in the back. The manager's wife, who had been tied up, went white, but she didn't cry out. Afterwards she fainted, which is why it took so long for the crime to be reported.

The two men fled with the bags, and when they reached a remote spot, they stopped to catch their breath. They were in a field. In the distance was a row of scattered lights. The black area before them must have been the lake. In spite of the urgency of the moment, Hikosuke felt the beauty of the scene.

After dividing the money by the flame of a lighter, they made a vow.

"This is the end of our relationship. From now on, we're like two complete strangers. We will never contact each other, not even to write a postcard. Neither of us will know the other's new address." This they solemnly swore to.

All at once, Hikosuke was seized by a chilling presentiment of doom, which led him to blurt out what he said next.

"Takeji, you're younger than I am, so you've got a lot more to enjoy in life. But from what I can gather from the newspapers, spending money wildly is a dead give-away. Women especially are taboo. Save your romancing for later, and use this money as capital to quietly start a business. No good will come from carrying on with women."

Takeji snickered in the darkness.

"I was thinking the same thing. A middle-aged man's love affairs are dangerous. You watch out yourself."

He was speaking softly as he always did, but his voice had a threatening ring to it.

"It's a relief to hear you say that. Be really careful then."

They shook hands and parted. Takeji's hand felt cold. Or was it that his own hand was burning?

Five years passed by. The police had conducted a thorough investigation of the robbery at the time but hadn't come up with anything.

Hikosuke quit his job and returned to Fukuoka, his home town. Using his two-million-odd yen as capital, he quietly began his current legitimate business. In the third year he decided it was safe to start advertising more. There were two reasons for this: one was that his business was growing steadily and showed promise; the other was that he was now confident no one would question the source of his capital. His three years of honest trade had given him a good reputation.

He had another important reason for feeling secure. He had no knowledge whatsoever of Takeji's whereabouts. Every day Hikosuke had scoured the papers, worried he'd find an article about Takeji's arrest for some crime or other. This, more than anything else, had preyed on his mind. Takeji's unstable character would seem to justify such fears, and if he was arrested, he might confess to this other, much more serious crime.

But the fears proved groundless. Takeji's name never appeared in the newspapers, and Hikosuke heard nothing at all about him. This was a good sign, for it meant that he was living a peaceful life somewhere. Probably Takeji had also used his capital to start some small legitimate business. When Hikosuke thought this far, all his anxieties were swept away. His business had been especially successful in the past two years because he had been able to concentrate totally on his work without letting anything disturb him.

Recently, however, he had once again begun to be haunted by anxiety.

3

Business was flourishing, his assets were sizable, and he had established both trust and social standing as a Fukuoka merchant. Just when he realized how far he had come and felt he could sit back and enjoy the best life had to offer, he was assaulted by a new and powerful fear—a fear stemming from the reality that Takeji was undoubtedly still alive somewhere in the world.

A wide range of crimes can be committed by one person working alone. The more accomplices there are, the higher the chances of failure. He knew from reading newspaper articles how often criminals were caught through the confessions of accomplices. But what preyed on Hikosuke's nerves now was different. It was the fear that the money he had amassed might lay him open to blackmail by his former accomplice. Before his present success, such worries had never entered his head. But once he had acquired wealth and a solid position, he was obsessed by this new fear of never knowing when he might be blackmailed.

He had money, trust, and status, and these could all survive a business slump. But not so with blackmail by the accomplice who held the secret to his past. He had amassed a fortune, but his life was in the hands of this man. Once the blackmail started, it was sure to continue until his hard-earned fortune had been sucked completely dry. The glum-faced Takeji seemed perfectly capable of such a course of action.

Hikosuke couldn't rid himself of the thought that one of these days Takeji, who was out there somewhere, would learn of his success and come after him, his eyes gleaming. *Out there somewhere.* Where, he did not know, but one day Takeji was sure to sniff out Hikosuke's fortune and show up, gloomy face and all. Where was Takeji, and what was he doing? Gradually this began to weigh heavily on Hikosuke.

Up until then he had felt only relief that he had no knowledge of Takeji's whereabouts. Now this very ignorance had begun to eat away at him. It was fear of the unknown, the panic felt when one does not know where an enemy's attack will come from.

Recently Hikosuke, who was nearing fifty, had taken a mistress, his first affair. Careful not to let his wife find out, he had built a house for his mistress and would visit her there. He was in love with her, so he was happy beyond measure. But this happiness, too, would collapse the moment Takeji appeared. When it came right down to it, his mistress was only attracted to his money.

Someday, thanks to Takeji, all his happiness would be taken from him. Hikosuke felt doomed. He became edgy; his nerves were frayed; he was unable to sleep at night.

"Darling, what's wrong? You're so pale and you always seem so depressed. You might be heading for a breakdown," said his pretty mistress. "You're working too hard. Relax at a hot spring and I know you'll feel better. I'll come with you," she coaxed him. If only that were the problem! He couldn't tell her the real reason.

But it was too early to despair. He decided to follow her advice. He went to stay at a hot spring inn called Funagoya, and while he was bathing there he had an inspiration. To what could he attribute this brilliant idea, which came to him suddenly out of the blue? Surely it was a revelation from heaven, as people used to say. Later, that was how it seemed to him.

When Hikosuke jumped energetically out of the bath, the water cascaded over the sides like a waterfall.

4

"My home town is Utsunomiya," Takeji had once let slip to Hikosuke. The key to his idea came from remembering this one sentence.

It might well be that Takeji was living in Utsunomiya, Hikosuke thought. After all, he himself had returned to his home town, Fukuoka. If he followed this line of reasoning, he could also surmise that Takeji had started a business in Utsunomiya.

This conjecture was based on the similarity in their circumstances. Their original situations were identical. There was every likelihood that Takeji had followed the same course of action as himself.

He quickly returned to Fukuoka and immediately dialed Directory Assistance.

"I'd like you to check the Utsunomiya area for a Takeji Machida. Is there any listing under that name?"

It took the operator a while before she replied that there was. Hikosuke's heart missed a beat.

"Oh, there is? Wh–What business is it?" His excitement made him stutter.

"It says 'lacquerware.' "

"Lacquerware? And his address?"

He jotted down what the operator said and then folded his arms, his mind a blank. The fact that it was exactly as he had predicted had paradoxically left him dazed.

So Takeji had opened a shop in Utsunomiya. Just like Hikosuke, Takeji had used the money from the bank robbery as capital to start a business in his home town. The two of them had acted in an identical fashion.

For the moment Hikosuke felt relieved. It was good news that Takeji had succeeded in his own way without any setbacks. There didn't seem much reason to worry about being blackmailed by him.

But when Hikosuke thought it over more carefully, he realized it was still too early for him to relax. Was Takeji's business going well? What was his life like now? What if his store was on the verge of bankruptcy, or he was leading a dissipated life? How could Hikosuke afford to ignore such possibilities? For if Takeji was in a situation where he was "pinched for money," he'd have a clear motive for blackmail.

Hikosuke realized the urgency of checking into Takeji's current situation. No, not just current. From here on, he'd have to watch over him. Who could say when his circumstances might change? It was vital that he be informed of each and every development.

Having thought this far, Hikosuke was able to feel peace of mind at last. It was the relief that came from spotting the enemy's hiding-place. Now he would have to turn this relief into something more substantial.

After several days of thought, Hikosuke put his plan into action. First he applied at the post office for a private box under the name "Business Information Services." Next, he got hold of the name of a local newspaper in Utsunomiya and sent the following "Help Wanted" ad.

> Looking for talented part-time reporter. Must be Utsunomiya resident. Good salary. Send photograph and résumé. Age: 25–40. Applicants will be notified by mail. Business

Information Services. Post Box No. XXX, Fukuoka Post Office.

The name "Business Information Services" implied that the company was putting out a trade paper without saying so directly—and that was enough.

He received a pile of résumés and photographs. He had forgotten how many unemployed there were in the world. Almost every applicant enclosed a letter detailing his own straitened circumstances.

Hikosuke hired one of them. From the photograph the man looked tactful and honest. He wore glasses but didn't seem smart-alecky. According to his résumé, he had graduated from a private university and been employed at a company, but he had had the bad luck to lose his job through a cutback in staff. His name was Ryoichi Takeoka. He was twenty-eight and was married.

Hikosuke sent off the following letter to his new reporter.

"Twice a month you are to report on the business activities and any unusual personal developments of the following Utsunomiya residents. It is essential that these parties remain unaware of your investigations. Your salary will be 15,000 yen a month and all correspondence should be limited to your reports."

He had requested information on three or four people, including Takeji. The others were merely names he had chosen at random from a business directory issued by a newspaper. These were decoys to dispel suspicion. All he really needed to know were the movements of one Takeji Machida.

It took a lot of hard thinking before Hikosuke came up with this plan. He had considered using a detective agency but realized that that wouldn't be sufficient. It would be necessary to employ somebody exclusively to keep a continuous watch over Takeji. But he had to make sure that the man he hired didn't get suspicious about his motives. That was why he had played it safe by advertising as what seemed to be the news service of a trade paper. It was also why he had requested reports on the other men.

Hikosuke believed that Takeji was now firmly in his grasp.

Nothing he did would ever escape his notice. His fear of the unknown had been removed. He'd be aware of every development in Takeji's life as it happened. And if Takeji started to sniff him out, he'd have plenty of time to think up some countermove. The reporter's monthly fee of 15,000 yen was nothing compared to the peace of mind it bought.

5

Ryoichi's first report arrived at the post box. The new reporter had gone about his job enthusiastically.

Hikosuke read the report carefully. He couldn't care less about the other people—Takeji's summary was the only one that mattered.

"Takeji Machida has a prosperous lacquerware business here, with assets estimated at roughly three million yen. He is somewhat of a loner and is not adept at dealing with people, but he has achieved a reputation for reliability in his business. He has a wife and two children. His hobby is playing *go*. He drinks moderately. There is no gossip of extramarital affairs."

This was the gist of the report.

Takeji's life seemed to be going smoothly. His being a loner and his ineptness at dealing with people matched his gloomy disposition. That was the only point that troubled Hikosuke, but it wasn't any big deal. There's always something to worry about if you look hard enough. Hikosuke praised Ryoichi for the quality of his report and asked him to continue sending the summaries.

When Hikosuke thought about it, this man Ryoichi Takeoka had hit upon a great job. For a mere two reports a month, he was receiving a salary of 15,000 yen.

It was only natural, then, for Ryoichi to be grateful. He wrote a long letter expressing his thanks, addressed to Hikosuke Uchibori, president of Business Information Services. The upshot was that he wanted to come from Utsunomiya to the main office in Fukuoka to introduce himself.

Hikosuke was flustered. It's not convenient for you to come;

it's not necessary; all you have to do is send accurate reports, he replied.

Ryoichi's reports were indeed accurate and detailed. Unfortunately, he also conducted thorough investigations on the other, extraneous men. In spite of his hard work, the summaries were of no interest or value to Hikosuke. But he couldn't very well have him stop. These decoys were a necessary precaution against Ryoichi finding out that Hikosuke was only interested in Takeji.

The reports continued. Two months passed, then three. There didn't appear to be any changes in Takeji's life. His business seemed to be going well. So far nothing to worry about.

Five months rolled by. Takeji, as he appeared in the reports, remained the same. It was a relief. Hikosuke and his former accomplice were living in completely separate worlds. They were two unconnected points, a great distance apart, independent of each other. Moreover, Hikosuke had a constant and clear knowledge of the other's circumstances.

However, Ryoichi, in all innocence, wrote another uncalled-for letter.

"I have already sent you ten reports, but I have still not received a copy of *Business Information*. Have all my reports been rejected? For future reference, I would greatly appreciate it if you could send me a copy of your paper."

There wasn't likely to be any such paper. Business Information Services didn't publish anything. Hikosuke angrily wrote the following reply.

"Our company's paper is published irregularly, only when necessary. At present there is no copy available. Do not concern yourself with what happens to your reports. Simply continue as you've been doing up until now."

After that, Ryoichi made no more requests. As directed, he faithfully continued his reports. Since he was receiving 15,000 yen every month, he had nothing to complain about.

At this point, what Hikosuke had secretly dreaded most began to appear in Ryoichi's reports. About six months had passed.

"Mr. Takeji Machida is keen on bicycle racing. He seems to be betting a lot of money, which is creating marital problems."

Hikosuke heart gave a lurch. His felt that his foreboding of doom was coming true.

After that, his premonition steadily began to become reality. One after another, the reports gave evidence of this.

"Mr. Machida has a mistress—this came to light recently. His marital problems are not only related to his gambling, it seems. Moreover, his business has taken an unexpected turn for the worse. He appears to be running it on high-interest loans. I was mistaken before when I wrote of the integrity of his business activities. I apologize for the inadequacy of my investigations."

The next report was as follows.

"Mr. Takeji Machida is on the verge of bankruptcy. Rumor has it that his store will be shut down soon."

The next three or four reports said more or less the same. Finally, this report came.

"Mr. Takeji Machida has lost his business. His store has been disposed of and he has left the city. According to rumor, he has opened a small lacquerware shop in Chiba City."

6

Hikosuke chewed on his nails nervously. Takeji had lost his business and had moved to Chiba. The situation was deteriorating rapidly. Hikosuke couldn't afford to let him out of his grasp.

Ryoichi continued to send detailed reports from Utsunomiya, but with Takeji no longer there, what was the point?

Hikosuke thought of discharging Ryoichi and looking for a new reporter in Chiba. He decided, though, that he'd be better off transferring the experienced Ryoichi. If he hired somebody new, there'd be no guarantee it would work out well. Ryoichi had his past record to back him up.

Ryoichi consented to the transfer to Chiba. Hikosuke had to pay the expenses for his sudden move, but there was no way of avoiding that.

About two weeks later, Ryoichi's reports from his new post

started coming in. As before, there was the unwanted news on other businessmen, but he didn't forget to report on the whereabouts of the all-important Takeji.

"Mr. Takeji Machida has been reduced to a petty merchant, a shadow of his former self. He appears to have brought his mistress with him. As always, his home life is full of friction. In my opinion, he won't be able to keep up even this small store. There seems to be no point in continuing the reports on Mr. Machida, but I await your instructions."

What he said made perfect sense. If Takeji had sunk so low, what use was he as the subject of a business report? But, conversely, what Hikosuke needed to know was Takeji's future movements. Now, more than ever, he had to keep track of him.

Hikosuke didn't know what to do. His camouflage was getting in the way, but he couldn't afford to worry about keeping it up any more. He sent Ryoichi a letter ordering him to pay special attention to Takeji's movements.

Ryoichi followed orders. His reports, without fail, contained news of Takeji.

Three months later came his report informing him of Takeji's downfall.

"Mr. Machida has closed his store and left Chiba. His wife has returned to her parents; he also seems to have broken up with his mistress. Mr. Machida's cousin lives here, and by chance I happened to become acquainted with him. He told me that Mr. Machida has gone to Osaka. He's virtually penniless. His cousin had to pay for his train fare. He has no idea what he'll do in Osaka. Before long, his cousin should receive news from him."

Takeji had been completely ruined. This was the situation that Hikosuke had feared more than anything. And at this critical stage, he had vanished from sight.

Hikosuke didn't give up hope. He couldn't, not now. Otherwise, what was the point of paying Ryoichi a monthly fee all this time to keep him posted on Takeji's whereabouts? It was now that he really needed to keep a watch over Takeji.

Hikosuke ordered Ryoichi to get information on Takeji's whereabouts from his cousin and then inform him in detail. He added by way of explanation that he wanted to use Takeji as a case study on the downfall of a businessman.

Ryoichi followed his instructions.

"According to his cousin, Mr. Machida is a day laborer in Osaka."

His next report: "Mr. Machida is working as a day laborer in Kobe."

For the next six months these reports continued.

"Mr. Machida has moved to Okayama. He's a coolie for a building contractor and is living at a construction camp."

"He's in Onomichi. His cousin doesn't know what he's doing there."

"He's gone to Hiroshima. He sent his cousin a postcard saying he's working as a laborer."

"He's in Yanai City in Yamaguchi Prefecture. It's not known what kind of work he's doing."

As the reports continued, the purpose behind Takeji's movements became apparent to Hikosuke. Takeji wasn't just roaming aimlessly. He had a clear goal. After leaving Chiba, he had been heading steadily west.

Why west? Because he was searching for his former accomplice, Hikosuke Uchibori.

Hikosuke had never told Takeji the name of his hometown. But he had mentioned vaguely that it was in the west. Surely he was searching for him, using that as a clue. Takeji would have also assumed that Hikosuke, a merchant by trade, had used the money to start his own business. He was wandering through the major cities in western Honshu, combing their shopping districts.

Hikosuke shuddered. Sometime, without fail, Takeji would come to Fukuoka. And then he would finally discover that his former partner in crime was now the owner of a highly successful furniture store.

7

Hikosuke was panic-stricken. He could feel the blood draining from his face. His head was spinning.

Takeji seemed to be wandering aimlessly, but the fact was that he was heading Hikosuke's way with unerring steps. There was no mistaking his direction. Hikosuke's ruin was approaching, slowly but surely.

What should he do? In any case, his business had grown far too big in Fukuoka to escape Takeji's notice.

No matter how he might resist, his destiny was closing in on him relentlessly.

"Mr. Takeji Machida is in Hofu City, Yamaguchi Prefecture."

"He's in Ube City."

"He's working as a laborer in Shimonoseki."

Ryoichi conscientiously continued his reports.

"He's in Kokura City. It's not clear what he's doing."

Takeji had finally come to Kyushu. He hadn't made one false move in his search for him. Hikosuke was so agitated that he could not sit still. The blood rushed to his head and he broke out in a cold sweat.

Another report arrived.

"Mr. Machida has been taken ill in Kokura City and can barely move. He's nothing better than a vagrant. He's built a makeshift hut at the foot of a lonely mountain and is living there by himself. His cousin showed me a letter from him and I made a note of where the hut is. I'm including this here for your reference."

Hikosuke covered his eyes. Suddenly his ears were assailed by a strange roaring. He got up and went somewhere quiet, thinking for a long time, his head in his hands.

He was about to lose all the happiness he had. The one man who could take it away from him was approaching steadily. Once Takeji arrived, Hikosuke would be forced to live out the rest of his life with the constant threat of having his bank robbery made public. If Takeji reached rock bottom, he'd be sure to pull down his rich accomplice with him. It could happen any time. Having lost both family and business, he'd try anything. Surely he'd be filled with hate and envy for his accomplice, who, in contrast to him, had managed to hold on to success.

"I'll suck him dry," Takeji must have resolved. That was why he was searching for him so relentlessly. He'd squeeze every penny out of Hikosuke. He'd probably consider it revenge on his successful accomplice. He had the power of life or death over Hikosuke, and he could tighten or loosen the noose as he pleased.

There must be some way to escape. Takeji was almost here. Hikosuke had to get free; he had to get out of the noose.

Hikosuke tugged at his hair as these desperate thoughts raced through his mind. His entire body felt burning hot. A long time passed.

At last he came up with an idea. Takeji was virtually an invalid in Kokura. He had become a vagrant; he was living alone in a mountain hovel. Luck was still on Hikosuke's side after all. "That's it," he shouted in relief.

He made some simple preparations. One night he went to a small hardware store at the edge of town and bought a pocketknife. No one would know who he was. It was an ordinary pocketknife, the kind a high school student would use. But it was going to save his life. One life would end, and one would be freed.

He told his family that he had some business to take care of. He planned it so that he'd arrive at Kokura around dusk.

When he got off at Kokura Station the sun was already setting. It was too dark to make out people's faces clearly. The timing was just right. The station was crowded with factory workers heading home. The conditions were perfect.

Hikosuke started walking. The mountain he was heading for stood black against the lingering daylight. He had a general idea where the place was, for he had lived in Kokura before and was well acquainted with the area.

A cold wind was blowing against his cheeks. His body was shaking, but it was not from the cold.

There were no more houses once he started climbing up the dark mountain. He could smell earth and dry leaves. He stopped to look around him. He was in the middle of a dark forest. He turned on his flashlight and doggedly went on.

8

It wasn't particularly difficult to find the hut. It took him thirty minutes. An old tin roof weighted down with rocks had been placed over some wooden boards.

For a while he stood in front of the entrance, over which straw matting had been hung. He had the weapon he had bought in his pocket. As he grasped it in his hand, his shaking ceased.

Hikosuke lifted up the matting and stepped inside. A foul odor assailed him—the stench of rotting fish and vegetables.

The tiny circle of light from the flashlight in his left hand revealed the shape of a man huddled under ragged bedding.

Once he got an idea of the layout of the room, he turned off the flashlight and called out to Takeji. He could sense the bedding shifting in the blackness.

"You're Takeji Machida, right?"

Hikosuke gripped the handle of his knife.

"Uh-huh."

The reply sounded almost like a moan in the darkness. Aiming at the voice, Hikosuke lunged.

The first thing he felt was the bedding. Then, from underneath, a great force came welling up. Hikosuke's body was sent flying as though propelled by a giant spring. He fell on his side. As he groped in the dark he was suddenly blinded by a beam of light. He couldn't open his eyes. The person holding the light burst into laughter. It was a young voice that did not bear the slightest resemblance to his memory of Takeji's voice.

"Who are you?" Hikosuke cried out in anger and fear.

"You came after all, Mr. Uchibori. I'm Ryoichi Takeoka, the man you hired," he said, controlling his laughter. He stood with his feet squarely planted.

"What? Ryoichi?" Hikosuke was shocked.

"I suppose I should say 'Nice to meet you,' but things have come to a strange pass." His voice was youthful yet composed. "I never thought it would end like this—when you hired me, that is. Oh, I've forgotten to express my thanks. I really am grateful.

23

You've helped me tremendously. And in return, it's come to this. I'm so sorry. It's all my fault. I've repaid your kindness with treachery. My curiosity is to blame. While I was sending you reports, I began to get wind of a crime."

The man who had introduced himself as Ryoichi seemed genuinely contrite. Hikosuke, strangely enough, was unable to move.

"First of all, you never sent me a copy of your newspaper, even though you claimed to be a business information service. I thought that a little odd, although at the time I didn't suspect anything. But when I reported that Mr. Machida moved to Chiba and you transferred me there, I began to get suspicious. I guessed it was Mr. Machida you were especially interested in. To make sure I wouldn't find out, you made me investigate the others. But once the important Mr. Machida moved to Chiba, your true intentions became clear. That was when I realized what my real function was—to keep watch over Mr. Machida and report his movements to you. You even ordered me to pay him special attention. I was sure I had it figured out right."

Ryoichi shifted slightly.

"Why, I wondered. What was the reason? My inborn love of detection took hold of me. I decided to do a test. I sent a false report saying that Mr. Machida had left Chiba."

"False, you say?" Hikosuke couldn't help shouting.

"Forgive me. In reality, Mr. Machida is still in Chiba. All this time he's been running his small lacquerware shop. But you immediately fell for my trick. You urgently ordered me to find out his whereabouts from his cousin and keep you posted. I could almost see the color draining from your face. There isn't any cousin, of course. I continued sending my fictitious Mr. Machida in the direction of Kyushu, and each time you demanded more detailed information. Your orders reeked of desperation. A-ha, this was something serious. It occurred to me that this something serious might be related to a crime."

There was a faint sound outside, but Ryoichi kept on talking.

"Not long ago, I hired a detective agency to investigate the identities of Mr. Machida and the owner of the private post office box in Fukuoka. As a result, I learned the present situation of both of you, but found out nothing about your pasts. But I did discover that even though your businesses are now different, formerly you were both traveling salesmen who worked around the country. This could be just coincidence, of course, but, as if by mutual agreement, you both quit your jobs to start your current businesses at exactly the same time six years ago.

"Most important, both of you started your businesses with a fair amount of capital, and neither of you borrowed the money. There was just a little too much coincidence. Something wasn't right. There was something here, some secret that the two of you shared. What's more, you hired me to keep a watch on Mr. Machida, and then eagerly had me follow his movements. I realized that you were frightened of him. My guess was that you were afraid he'd blackmail you. My reasoning turns out to have been flawless.

"I rushed to Kokura from Chiba, made preparations, and then sent you the letter saying that Mr. Machida was living here in Kokura. Then I waited. If you had looked carefully at the postmark, you'd have noticed it was sent from Kokura, not Chiba. I was convinced you'd show up here in search of Mr. Machida. You were scared out of your wits by him. All because of some secret between the two of you. You might even try to kill him if you could. With that in mind, I created the scenario, and then lay in wait for you.

"With no evidence, there was nothing for the police to investigate. To start an investigation, I had to lure you into committing some crime, and then catch you in the act. My plan worked well. You assaulted me with a weapon. Please forgive me. Oh, *they*'ll be here in a moment. They'll find out soon enough what I still don't know. . . about you and Mr. Machida."

With these words, Ryoichi gave a whistle. From the dark undergrowth outside, the stirring of footsteps could be heard.

The Face

For the sake of simplicity, all the dates in this diary have been omitted. While the entries are in chronological order, the intervals between each are extremely irregular—one day, four days, a week, even a month. The reader can gauge how much time has elapsed between each from the contents of the entries.

FROM THE DIARY OF RYOKICHI INO

After the dress rehearsal today, the principal members of our theater group stayed behind to discuss something. I left with A., and we chatted as we walked to Gotanda Station.

"Do you know what the meeting's about?"

I shook my head.

"T. Movie Company is negotiating with us over roles in their next film," A. explained. "It'll be directed by the famous Ishii, who wants three or four supporting actors from our group. In the last few weeks our manager Y. has been going to the movie company any number of times."

"I had no idea. Are we going to do it then?" I asked.

"You bet we are. We're in bad shape, you know, in the red for God knows how long. Y. is hoping that this will turn into a perma-

27

nent arrangement—if the other side agrees to it, that is."

A. was always in the know when it came to goings-on in the group.

"Did the initial offer come from us?"

"No, from the movie company, but it doesn't seem to be coughing up a lot of money. They'll be paying around one million three hundred thousand yen for the four of us. Still, it all helps."

"Who are they going to pick?"

Even as I asked I was mulling over the potential candidates, and the names mentioned by A. were the very people I thought most likely.

"Movies are good publicity. And it'll help make a name for our group as well."

We had a drink together at a cheap bar by the station.

***

I've had an unexpected request from our manager, Y. He wants me to be one of the four in T. Company's next film. The other three, I found out, were all leading actors of the group.

"Why this stroke of luck?" I asked.

"The director, Ishii, singled you out," Y. explained. "He saw our production of *Immorality* and was taken with your performance. He says he definitely wants you in his movie."

The newspaper reviews for *Immorality* had praised me: "Newcomer Ryokichi Ino gave an excellent performance, breathing life into his role of the nihilistic youth." Reaction had been favorable within the group as well. Still, in the final analysis, the role had been a minor one. I hardly expected to be the focus of so much attention.

"Ishii is well known for being a perfectionist. He feels that the actors in the company aren't right for the roles in *Spring Snow*. Your part is a small one, with only a few scenes, but he insists on using you. So we all discussed it and gave our consent. The group needs the money. We want our own theater so we won't have to rent halls constantly. And, most important of all, it will be good for your career."

Y. was absolutely correct. I joined The White Willow Players less than eight years ago. This could be the lucky break I've been waiting for.

"I'll give it my best."

I bowed slightly. I wasn't unhappy. Far from it, I was quite excited. But at the same time a certain feeling of uneasiness crept over me.

Inadvertently this must have showed in my face. Y. patted me on the shoulder.

"It'll be all right. Unlike plays, movies are made up of lots of small scenes—hack acting. It's nothing to get nervous about," he encouraged.

He has it wrong. My uneasiness is of an entirely different nature. Something much more ominous.

***

Filming for *Spring Snow* has begun. When acting in a play, I never get nervous, but just the thought of a film is enough to make me jumpy. And for good reason, too. The White Willow Players perform only to small select audiences within the city, but this movie will be seen by large numbers of people all over the country. And I won't have any idea *who* might go and see it. When they told me that the filming will be wrapped up soon, apprehension swept over me like a black, malevolent cloud. If I tried telling this to anybody, it would only be misinterpreted as fears about how my performance will be judged.

Ishii is a sensitive director. He seems to have taken a liking to me.

***

All my scenes are finished. With a director as famous as Ishii, the movie has attracted a lot of attention and advance publicity.

I've received my share of the fees. According to Y., almost all of the one million two hundred thousand yen finally agreed on by the film company will go into the group's funds. I got forty thousand yen out of it, which was fine by me. Recently, I've been able to buy whatever takes my fancy as well as to invite A. to the more fashionable drinking spots in Shibuya. A. seems jealous of my

29

luck. I've almost reached a point in my career where others might envy me.

I drank much more than usual tonight, and it wasn't through happiness. I was trying to drown this gnawing apprehension.

***

I saw the coming attractions for *Spring Snow,* but none of my scenes was included. The advertisement said it was "coming soon." So it's finally going to be released. I can't help feeling afraid.

***

I saw a preview of *Spring Snow.* I couldn't focus on anyone's face but my own. Still, I appeared in just five or six scenes. There were two close-ups, but they only lasted a few seconds. I felt somewhat relieved.

***

The newspaper reviews for *Spring Snow* have been favorable. "Ryokichi Ino from The White Willow Players is superb. His vaguely nihilistic looks are most effective." All the reviewers seem to have picked on the same point. I appreciate the good notices, but . . .

***

Y. let me in on the comments he'd heard in various places.

"Ishii has spoken highly of you," he said with a big grin.

"Really?" I felt elated in spite of myself. "Y., I know a nice spot in Shibuya. Would you like to come for a drink?" I invited him out.

At the bar Y. said, "You've had a lucky break, so make the most of it." He patted me on the back.

I felt the same way. I was almost ecstatic. It seemed I'd be able to make a name for myself soon. I might even end up rich. Up until now I've been so poor. In a book I once read, a successful foreign actor said something like this: "After I made a lot of money, I didn't know how to spend it. I thought of hiding myself in a private room in a huge, fancy restaurant, sipping champagne and hiring my own gypsy to play for me. And I would listen to the music and sob."

I'm the kind of person who lets his fantasies get ahead of him.

I boarded the Yamanote Line for home, and when I looked out the train window at the scattered, dim lights around Harajuku, I felt the uneasiness once again. The happiness that was finally taking root had been slashed by a razor.

***

Two months have passed since the film went on general release throughout the country. He probably hasn't see it. Nothing's happened. But that's only to be expected. It would have been a one-in-ten-thousand, a one-in a-hundred-thousand coincidence.

***

T. Movie Company has made another offer, this time for me alone. Lady Luck's smiling at me. It's my big break!

Y. said to me, "They offered four hundred thousand yen, but we held out for five and they came around. They're really taken with you. The producer wants to meet you tonight. Can you make it?"

The meeting was held in a quiet private room in a Shimbashi restaurant. Both the producer and director were present. A contract was signed, with Y. acting as the witness.

"The screenplay is still being written. Production will start in about two months," said the tall, bespectacled producer. In two months. I thought vacantly of the time.

"I'm the one who insisted on you being in the film. In the screenplay there's a part for a man with a nihilistic character, and none of our own actors is right for it. But your looks are just perfect for the part." The fattish director grinned as he spoke.

"Is Ino's role a big one?" Y. asked.

"Oh, yes. This will make him famous. He has a peculiar appeal." The producer's eyes sparkled behind his glasses.

"There are no actors in Japan who have his kind of personality. Actors with pretty faces and no individualism won't be able to

31

land major roles much longer. The trend now is for talented actors who've been playing supporting roles to take over the leads."

The more I listened, the more I began to feel that I could really make it all happen. I was trembling with joy. I was floating on air. Incredible things were happening to me at an amazing speed.

***

I feel as if I'm walking headlong into good fortune—and disaster. My own despair is eating away at the very foundations of my happiness.

In the earlier movie, the chances of being noticed were one in ten thousand or one in a hundred thousand. With this film, my role is much more important and my face will appear in numerous scenes. If I become famous, I'll act in even more films. The chances of him seeing my face will multiply, to one in ten perhaps. Then the danger will no longer be a possibility but an inevitability.

I already fantasize about the fall that will follow on the heels of my success.

***

I want to make a grab for happiness. To be honest, I want fame and social standing. I want money. I want to have the kind of status that would allow me to listen to a hired musician and sob as I sip champagne in a plush restaurant. I refuse to give up the happiness I've worked so hard for.

***

Recently I've been obsessed with the thought of what might happen. I feel like an idiot. My nerves are too taut. There's no easy way out. I've started seriously considering taking some drastic measures.

***

They tell me that filming for *The Red Forest* will begin in thirty days. In sixty days it will be released throughout the country. Sixty days to the arrival of that cursed inevitability.

Sixty days. Before time runs out, I am resolved to do something to put an end to these fears once and for all. I'll do the dirty work myself. I have decided to "gamble."

***

I went drinking with Y.

"You know, the film company bought you because you have such a cold look. You have the kind of face that's popular among intellectuals these days."

He stared at me with the detached eyes of a painter.

"Do I really look so different?"

"Oh, yes, definitely. Your face has something peculiar about it."

Of late I have been hearing the same comments from the crew at the studio. The movie is clearly trying to sell my "face." In this way the face of a New Wave actor called Ryokichi Ino, until yesterday a complete unknown, is destined to become the center of attention of a gullible audience.

If it comes to that, there'll be virtually no escape from this inevitability.

***

It's been a long time since I've taken the eight manila envelopes out of the locked drawer. On the backs of all of them are printed the words, "P. DETECTIVE AGENCY." As I put in a request every year, this represents a total of eight years' worth. They all contain reports on the same person. For eight years, although I can hardly afford it, I've been forking out the high fees.

I took out the contents of the first envelope, the report I asked for eight years ago, in 1948.

"The investigations requested on Mr. Teizaburo Ishioka have been delayed due to our initial difficulty in ascertaining his address. However, basing our inquiries on your statement that he works in the iron and steel industry, we were finally able to track down his whereabouts, and have been able to complete the following report."

I had gone to a detective agency in Tokyo to seek information concerning a man called Teizaburo Ishioka, who lived in Yawata City in Kyushu. When the clerk asked me for his address, I told him I didn't know. When questioned about his place of work, I replied that I wasn't sure but I had heard that he worked in the iron and steel industry. The clerk remarked that it wasn't much of a lead, but as the company had a branch office in Kyushu, they would give it a try.

Leave it to the pros. What they had to go on was no more than the slenderest of threads, yet they were able to make headway with their inquiries. The principle points of the report were as follows. "Teizaburo Ishioka is an employee at Kita-Kyushu Steel Works. His present address is 3 Tori-cho, Yawata City. He was born in 1922, and is now twenty-six years old; he is single; his parents are deceased, and he has siblings living in his home town. For details, please refer to the enclosed copy of his family register. Mr. Ishioka's monthly salary is 9,000 yen. An extrovert, he is well thought of at work. He likes to go drinking. He doesn't smoke. His hobbies are mahjongg and fishing. There is no gossip concerning relations with women."

This was the first report; and I requested a new one every year. But for four years straight they contained nothing new.

In the fifth year there was a change: "He is now working at Y. Electrical Engineering Company's Kurosaki factory; his address has changed to 1 Honmachi, Kurosaki, Yawata City."

And two other small changes: in the sixth year, "He got married on March 20"; and in the seventh year, "A son has been born."

There was nothing new in the eighth report I received this year.

"Teizaburo Ishioka's present address is 1 Honmachi, Kurosaki, Yawata City. He is employed at Y. Electrical Engineering Company's Kurosaki factory; his salary is 17,000 yen. His wife is twenty-eight. His son is one."

In this way, I have kept track of the last eight years of a certain individual named Teizaburo Ishioka. The agency's fees are steep for me, but I have the satisfaction of keeping constant tabs on his circumstances.

I lined up the eight envelopes containing the documents and slowly smoked a cigarette.

Teizaburo Ishioka.

It was nine years ago when I came to know his name and face. To be exact, it was on June 18, 1947, inside a Sanin Line train that was running along the coast of Shimane Prefecture heading toward Kyoto. The incident lasted only about twenty minutes, from about 11:20 A.M., when the train left a small station called Tsuda, until it reached Hamada Station.

Miyako, who was sitting next to me, was bored with looking at the scenery, and suddenly spotted him among the passengers.

"Oh, it's Mr. Ishioka, isn't it?" she had called out. As we had boarded the train at the terminal in Shimonoseki, we had seats all the way. Those who had gotten on in mid-journey were standing.

"Hey," a young man shouted from among the crowd. He was in his mid-twenties, with a dark complexion, thick lips, and bulging eyes.

"Miyako? You're the very last person I expected to see here. What a shock!"

He really did look surprised. He stole a casual glance at me in the seat next to her. I stared out the window, smoking a cigarette and acting indifferent, one eye half-closed, smarting from the smoke.

"I take it you're on a food hunt." Miyako's tone was unabashedly lively. In those early postwar days, food in the cities was in short supply, so you had to go to the country to buy things.

"When you're single," said Ishioka, "you'll always have enough food to get by. Actually, I come from around here. I've taken a short holiday to rest up and eat my fill. I'll probably head back to Yawata tomorrow or so. Tell me, what are *you* doing here?"

"Me? I'm looking for food! Compared to Kita-Kyushu, they say Shimane Prefecture is loaded with stuff."

Miyako, perhaps noticing that the nearby passengers were laughing to themselves at her comment, added, "But, in fact, it doesn't matter if I can't find anything good. I'm just going to relax at a hot spring, and I'll pick something up on the way back if I can."

"A hot spring? I really envy you!"

Once more Ishioka seemed to look me over. Clearly he had figured out that I was with her. I continued to stare out the window.

Miyako and Ishioka chatted on about this and that. At last the train pulled into Hamada Station.

"Well, so long. I'll drop by the bar when I get back to Yawata."

"I'll be expecting you. Goodbye."

Ishioka pushed through the crowd, elbowing his way to the door. It may have been my imagination, but he seemed to turn and stare at my face again before getting off.

Miyako and I had been riding trains all the way from Yawata, journeying through Kyushu and then continuing on to Honshu. But until we got to Honshu we had purposely sat apart from each other to avoid being noticed. Miyako, a hostess in a cheap bar, had explained that she didn't want us to be seen by anybody. This arrangement suited my own purposes, too, so I was furious with her for calling out to an acquaintance near the end of our trip, despite all our efforts to make sure we weren't spotted by anyone we knew. When I reproached her, she retorted, "But he's one of my customers and a good-natured fellow. I was so surprised to see him that I couldn't help calling out to him. Don't worry. He's not the type to bad-mouth me." I could guess what she was hinting at.

"He's interested in you then?"

Miyako tilted her head self-consciously and smiled coquettishly.

I realized that something critical had happened. The incident had lasted a mere fifteen or twenty minutes, but he had seen us together and my plan was fouled up.

"What's his name?" I was insistent.

"Teizaburo Ishioka. That's what he told me."

Teizaburo Ishioka. Commit it to memory, I thought. From the very start, his name was etched on my brain.

"Where does he work?"

"I'm not sure. He once said something about working in the iron and steel industry."

"Where does he live?"

"I don't know. Hey, what are you thinking? Are you jealous?" Miyako pursed her lips, then gave a vulgar, ugly laugh that revealed her gums.

The more I thought about it, the more heavily it weighed on me that for fifteen or twenty minutes on the Sanin Line train a man called Teizaburo Ishioka had seen Miyako and me together. Why did she have to call out to him? Frustration and anger assailed me on all sides, like germs invading a small, festering wound.

No third party had ever been a witness to our relationship. Not once had I shown my face at Miyako's bar. Since she lived on the premises, I'd invent some name or other whenever I telephoned, and we'd always meet outside. Our rendezvous were usually in cheap inns that we switched constantly. We had met while buying food in the countryside and no one knew us there. In short, ours had been a secret relationship until this last, crucial moment when we were spotted together by Ishioka. He had stared at me. There was no chance he'd forget my face—this face that everyone says is so "peculiar"!

I, too, could clearly recall his face with its bulging eyes and thick lips. I only had to see the name Teizaburo Ishioka and that face would rise up in front of me. For the first nine months, however, Ishioka's existence elicited no more than a slight anxiety in me. I had come to Tokyo with the hope of finding acting work and soon after had joined The White Willow Players.

To tell the truth, I felt that I had been worrying needlessly. What did it matter, having been seen by him? I was trying desperately to convince myself that he hadn't noticed anything, that there was no reason to worry.

But I was soon to discover that such wishful thinking was mere self-deception. . . .

***

(*Continued from yesterday.*) It was the end of September. I had come to Tokyo in July. Many things are available in a big city, and in the downtown Yurakucho area provincial newspapers from around the country are on sale for those who miss news of their home towns. I'd go there every day to pick up papers from Kita-Kyushu and Shimane Prefecture. Toward the end of September the article I was waiting for appeared in the Shimane paper.

"On September 26, around 10 A.M., the partly decomposed body of a woman was found by a villager in the forests near Okuni Village in Nima County. According to the report from the Omori Police Department, the autopsy showed evidence of strangulation. From her clothing, et cetera, her age is estimated at twenty-one or twenty-two. A search to determine her identity and that of the murderer has begun. The victim does not seem to have been a local resident."

One month later, toward the end of October, the following article appeared in the local Kita-Kyushu paper.

"The corpse of Miyako Yamada (21), a hostess at the Hatsu-hana Bar in Chuo Ward, Yawata City, was discovered in the mountains of Okuni Village in Nima County, Shimane Prefecture. Death was due to strangulation. The police had been conducting a search for Yamada, who had been missing since June 18. After notification by the Omori Police Department, someone was immediately sent to identify the body. It is not clear why Yamada had gone to that area, but police believe that she was taken there and murdered. On June 18, around 11 A.M. Yamada was seen on the Kyoto-bound Sanin Line, traveling with a man. Yawata police suspect this man to be the murderer and are conducting a search based on a description of him."

It didn't surprise me very much that Miyako's corpse had been discovered. But the news in the Kita-Kyushu paper that a witness had seen Miyako and a male companion riding the Sanin Line was, in spite of its probability, a shock. Resigned as I was, icy fingers seemed to clutch at my heart. It goes without saying that the witness was Teizaburo Ishioka.

So he had known after all! The faint hope I had nurtured that he might not have noticed me was shattered. Undoubtedly, he would have given the police a detailed description of the man accompanying Miyako.

"If you saw him again, would you be able to identify him?" the policeman would have asked.

"Sure, I remember his face clearly. I could identify him with one eye shut," Ishioka had no doubt asserted. During those twenty minutes on the train, he must have committed to memory every single feature of my face.

On the pretext of a "hot spring vacation," I had deliberately lured Miyako away from Yawata and killed her in the remote Sanin mountains. I had chosen the spot for its isolation, as the place least likely to be searched. Just my luck that, in spite of all my precautions, *he* would board the same train just as we were approaching our journey's end.

When I thought about it later, I realized that I should have postponed my plan at that point. We had run into someone she knew, so to be on the safe side I should have rescheduled the whole thing. But there was no holding my feelings back at that time. They pressed in on me so much that I had no way to escape. I couldn't put it off. I had to be free of Miyako as quickly as possible.

She was pregnant. And no matter what I said, she refused to have an abortion.

"There's no way you can talk me into it. I couldn't do anything so cruel to my first child. You want me to have an abortion so you can leave me. Coward! Well, you're not going to have it so easy. What makes you think you can be so selfish? I'll follow you to the ends of the earth."

I regretted ever getting involved with such an uncouth, loud-mouthed woman—stuck-up, too, in spite of her ugliness. I had tried to break with her, but she was tenacious. After getting pregnant, she became even more so. When I thought of the life I'd spend with the child she'd bear, I almost blacked out in despair.

Why should my life be ruined by this vile woman? Could there be anything more irrational, more ridiculous? In anger I made a vow to myself: if Miyako wouldn't part of her own will, then I would have no choice but to kill her to set myself free. I couldn't stand the misery of spending my whole life with a worthless woman simply because of one tiny mistake. Whatever it took, I had to fling her aside and live again.

In this way I resolved to murder Miyako. She was delighted when I suggested a trip to a hot spring.

Fortunately, we had kept our relationship a secret from the beginning, so even if Miyako disappeared, or if her body was discovered, no one would be able to link us. I was a mere stranger in the crowd.

Aside from bumping into Ishioka on the train, everything had gone smoothly. Miyako and I spent a night in a place called Yunotsu. The following day we walked into a deserted forest in the mountains. As I caressed her amidst the stifling aroma of luxuriant midsummer vegetation, I strangled her.

I returned to Yawata, collected my belongings, and decided to fulfill my long-cherished goal of going to Tokyo. No one would take any notice of the movements of one man among the teeming multitudes.

The one and only person in this world who would think of linking me to Miyako was the witness Ishioka—no, not just "think," for he had notified the authorities.

"Miyako was traveling with a man when she was murdered in the Sanin area. I saw him on the train."

He was the only one who had seen my face!

***

(*Continued from yesterday.*) Ever since that newspaper article, I have exercised extreme caution regarding Teizaburo Ishioka. I've been almost morbidly careful. It was because I wanted to keep track of his whereabouts that I had hired the detective agency every year to make a report on him. It was a relief to know that he had settled down in Yawata City. As long as he remained in Kyushu, I was safe in Tokyo.

However, something unforeseen happened: I got a role in a movie. My face would be on screens all over the country. If Ishioka saw it, he would jump out of his seat. What guarantee did I have that he wouldn't go to the movie?

When I first appeared in *Spring Snow* I felt as if I was walking on thin ice. The fear that he might see me had turned my nerves to jelly. When nothing happened, I breathed more easily.

But with *The Red Forest* things will be different. There's no comparing the size of my role. The movie company is trying to sell *me*. The probability that Ishioka will recognize my face in the movie has become a virtual certainty.

For my own protection, I should have refused the movie role point-blank. And yet how could I have turned down this long-awaited good fortune? I want to get the best out of life. I want fame and fortune. I want to make my ambitions come true.

***

Today I received a copy of the script. I can tell at a glance that my role is a major one with lots of scenes and close-ups.

Shooting will begin in a week.

I have to do something quickly.

***

Last night I could hardly sleep. In my head I churned over innumerable stratagems.

Ishioka's existence is the only anxiety I have in the world. I have to do something to dispel it or else I'll go crazy. I have already decided what I must do, for I have to protect myself. For the sake of my ambition, I will stop skulking and take the offensive.

What I'm concerned with now is not what I must do but how to carry it off. I'm cowardly enough to fear failure. But then it would just be a case where a little-known actor named Ryokichi Ino disappears. Even so, I'm gambling with my life.

***

I spent the whole day thinking. I'm exhausted.

***

The director has suddenly taken on a movie project for the Kyoto studio. Shooting here will be delayed two months.

Things are turning out well.

Tonight, on my way back from a rehearsal of my group, I stopped at a bookstore and picked up a detective novel. I got bored and gave up halfway. My resolution to summon Ishioka has hardened.

***

Here's what I have thought of so far.

1. The place should be deserted and isolated, possibly in the mountains, but it will be difficult to lure him there without arousing his suspicions. The hard part is coming up with a good plan. Using a third party would involve an accomplice, a weak spot that could spell potential trouble and to be avoided.

2. Potassium cyanide is a good method. Should be easy to pour it into his drink unnoticed. Will proceed as the circumstances allow.

3. How to get him there. He has to come alone and, most important, I need to be completely assured that he *will* come. There's no point if he doesn't respond.

The above conditions must all be met.

***

I've decided that a secluded forest or wood in the mountains is ideal since there'll be no chance of being spotted. For that reason, a beach or level land is out. A building also has drawbacks; there's always the danger of being seen entering or leaving.

It must be a place where we could be spotted climbing a mountain and attract no attention. A place where we could encounter someone on the way and arouse no suspicion.

***

Today, while waiting for a train at Ochanomizu Station, the travel advertisements put out by the railways caught my eye.

Gazing unthinkingly at posters for Mt. Takao, Mitake, Nikko, and other famous tourist spots, I had an inspiration: if it is a tourist area, we will attract no one's attention, even if we are riding on trains or walking in the streets. I am obsessed with this idea.

***

I've definitely decided it has to be a tourist spot. After mulling it over again this morning, it still seems the best plan.

Now, for the actual place.

I have picked the Kyoto region, halfway between Tokyo and his home in Yawata, Kyushu. A wild notion perhaps, but won't calling him to a distant place have the opposite effect of what one might expect, and actually inspire trust? Conversely, a place closer to home would probably be dismissed as a practical joke.

I'll send him the money for the train fare and a night's lodging. Four thousand yen should be sufficient. One can't overestimate the psychological effect of money for instilling trust and ruling out the idea that it's a practical joke. In this case, the money will lend credibility to the letter I plan to send.

If he has any interest in the incident, he will come without fail. After all, he's the only person who can identify the murderer.

The place I have chosen is Mt. Hiei.

I have been there twice before and know it fairly well. The entire mountainside is covered with dense forests of cedar and cypress. The cable car route from Sakamoto to the temple of Konponchu-do at the top of the mountain is a well-known pilgrimage route. Two people walking together will not arouse any suspicion. Even if the body is discovered later, I doubt there'll be anybody who'll even remember his face.

Besides Konpon-chudo there are various temple buildings scattered about the mountainside—Dai-kodo, Kaidan-in, Jodo-in, et cetera. As we walk up the mountain, we'll look as if we are taking in the sights; no one will give us a second thought. There is one path leading to Shimeidake and another to Saito; both are heavily forested.

I have found the place.

***

I took the night train to Kyoto.

Every aspect of the plan has to be worked out carefully. Such attention to detail is essential.

I got on a train to Sakamoto and toward noon boarded the cable car up Mt. Hiei. I wanted to get a good grasp of the area in advance. This was one of the two reasons I had come to Kyoto.

The cable car was nearly empty. The end of March was still early for viewing cherry blossoms or for the spring foliage that follows them. Thanks to the good weather I had a pretty view of Lake Biwa in the distance. I made my way leisurely to Konpon-chudo. Most of the passengers from the cable car were with me. We passed only a few people coming the other way.

Kaidan-in was a bit farther up from Dai-kodo. I sat down facing it and slowly smoked five cigarettes. Actually, I was looking the area over. The path from Kaidan-in led uphill, where in one direction it branched off to Saito, and in another to the Yase cable car station, passing through Shimeidake. But after watching the area for nearly an hour, I noticed that virtually everyone—whether tourists or pilgrims—headed back after visiting Konpon-chudo and Dai-kodo. Almost no one seemed to go on toward Saito or Shimeidake.

Good, that settles it. I will take the path toward Saito.

The track was uphill and narrow. There wasn't a soul in sight. Inside the cedar groves, small old temple buildings with names like Shaka-do and Ruri-do lay deserted, as if they had been discarded in the shadows of the early spring light. As I went farther, the buildings disappeared, and in their place a deep, thickly wooded valley cast a numbing quietude. Bush warblers sang intermittently. I stopped to light a cigarette. Before I had smoked it, I spotted a priest in a black kimono, like a shadow in the midday sun, coming down the narrow path I was walking up. As he passed me, I asked him if there were any temples farther up.

"The Dragon Temple of Kurodani," the priest muttered and continued wearily down the path.

The Dragon Temple of Kurodani. I could picture what it looked like from its name. It seemed fitting that there should be such a temple at the end of this lonely mountain path.

I remained in the area a while longer, alternately standing still and wandering about until the lay of the land was fixed in my mind.

However, at that time I still didn't have any concrete plan. This occurred to me only after I had taken the cable car down and noticed a newly built apartment house by the side of Hiyoshi Shrine. When I spotted bedding, blankets, and white sheets being aired outside the windows, like episodes in the lives of the residents, the idea came to me. I worked out the details on the train back to Kyoto.

At my inn that evening, I spent a long time composing the following letter.

Dear Mr. Ishioka,

Please forgive me for writing to you out of the blue. I am a relative of Miyako Yamada. Nine years ago, Miyako, who was working at the Hatsuhana Bar in Yawata, was taken to the countryside in Shimane Prefecture and murdered. I believe you are aware of this. I am a salesman for a tableware manufacturer in Nagoya; I spend the better part of the year making the rounds of large stores and restaurants in all parts of the country. I am writing to you now from an inn in Kyoto. Recently I noticed a man working at a grocery store here whom I suspect is Miyako's murderer. He is originally from Shimane Prefecture, and nine years ago was living in Yawata, Kyushu. There are other reasons why I am convinced that he is the murderer, but I would prefer to fill you in on the details when we meet. This brings me to the point of my letter. It seems that in a Sanin Line train near the place Miyako was killed, you happened to see her with the murderer. I would very much like you to come and look at the suspect's face, for you are the only one who is able to identify him. If you confirmed my suspicions, we could immediately present our case to the police. My suspicions alone are not sufficient as evidence; it is your identification that will be decisive. I sincerely apologize for the inconvenience, but four days from now, on April 2, I will be expecting you at 2:30 P.M. in the waiting room of Kyoto Station. I will be wearing a light brown cap and glasses, so when you spot me, please call to me. I am sorry for arbitrarily deciding on the day, but I will be leaving for an extended business trip in northern Japan that evening and would like to see you before then if at all possible. Please accept the enclosed money order for your transportation.

I am firmly convinced that the man I suspect is guilty, but I can't do anything without your evidence. I am withholding his name out of respect for his rights in the very unlikely case that I am proved wrong. For the same reason, please refrain from contacting the police. If it becomes necessary, the police here will serve the purpose.

I know how unreasonable this request is, but I am sure you can understand my feelings in wanting to bring to justice the despicable man who murdered Miyako. I implore you to respond affirmatively.

> Sincerely,
> Riichi Umetani

I read the letter over any number of times, then breathed a sigh of relief. The proximity of the appointed date and the return address as "an inn in Kyoto"—appropriate for someone traveling— were stratagems to prevent an inquiring reply. Moreover, it wouldn't do for the envelope to have a Tokyo postmark. That was the other reason I had come to Kyoto.

I chose the waiting room at Kyoto Station for our rendezvous because it is the least likely place to put him on guard. The brown cap and glasses will, of course, be part of my disguise. And when it comes down to it, I plan to make full use of my acting skills and makeup to change my expression.

When I sent the registered letter together with a 4,000 yen money order from the post office in front of Kyoto Station, I sensed that a life-or-death battle had just begun.

Will Ishioka really come? This doubt hardly troubles me. Of course he will come! I am absolutely convinced of this.

***

Last night I boarded the train back to Tokyo. As I swayed back and forth with the rhythm of the train, I went over my plan again and again, making sure that I had overlooked nothing, that it could be carried out without a hitch. It is just like rehearsing before the opening of a play.

First, I will go to the waiting room of Kyoto Station at 2:30 P.M. on the appointed day. A man will stand up on seeing my brown cap. It will be Ishioka, with his thick eyebrows and bulging eyes. Probably the following scenario will take place.

"Excuse me, are you Mr. Umetani?" he asks. He politely explains that he has taken the night train from Kyushu and arrived this morning. My hat, glasses, and the rest of my disguise will prevent him from recognizing me.

"Thank you for making such a long trip." I greet him affably. "Well, shall we get going right away? I have just checked on his whereabouts and was told he's taken the day off. But don't worry, I have his home address. Do you mind if it's a bit out of the way? Where is it, you ask. Sakamoto, just under an hour from here by train. Shall we go then?" After an exchange of this sort, we board the train to Otsu.

At Hamaotsu we change to a train running by the lake.

"That's Lake Biwa."

"What a nice view."

The man from Kyushu cranes toward the window in admiration.

We get off at Sakamoto. When we climb the hill toward Hiyoshi Shrine we can see a white apartment house on the right.

"That's it. That's where he lives," I point out. Ishioka's thick eyebrows twitch nervously.

"Please wait here. I'll go up to his apartment and lure him out. Then look over his face carefully. Whether you recognize him or not, just act indifferent. We'll stand there talking briefly and then he'll probably go back into the building. If it is him, we can contact the police immediately."

He nods in agreement. I leave him and enter the building. I don't knock on anyone's door; I simply wait awhile and then return. Ishioka is standing in the same spot, looking somewhat tense and nervous.

"A bit of bad luck," I say. "He's not home. According to his wife, he's not feeling well and has gone to see the doctor. That's why he took the day off. She told me the doctor's in Kyoto so it'll be another two hours before he gets back. Why don't we wait?"

Having come all the way from Kyushu, he's sure to agree to this.

"Since we've got two hours to kill, how about going up Mt. Hiei? The cable car is right here. Have you ever been to Konpon-chudo?"

He'll most likely reply that he hasn't. Even if he's been there before, I doubt he'll refuse my invitation.

The two of us board the cable car. Lake Biwa recedes quickly into the distance as the view opens out before us. The surface of the far side of the lake is shrouded in a spring mist.

"It's nice, isn't it?"

"Wonderful!"

All reserve has broken down. We arrive at the station on top of the mountain and take the winding path through the wood to Konpon-chudo. At this point he might ask me questions.

"How did you figure out that the man living there is Miyako's murderer?"

I give various plausible explanations. It's child's play. He agrees to everything I say, never suspecting anything.

We soon reach Konpon-chudo. We admire the vermilion lacquered edifices scattered in the cedar grove. I pick up two bottles of soda or juice and two cups at a stall and we climb farther up the hill.

"Let's take in Saito. It's not very far."

He follows me. From here on there are very few tourists. It's just the two of us, walking slowly. We look at Shaka-do and Ruri-do, and then continue up the quiet road.

"There's a temple called the Dragon Temple of Kurodani farther up. We can walk there and then come back. We have just enough time," I explain. The longer we walk, the fewer signs there are of other people. Forests of cedar and cypress cover the valley slopes.

"Why don't we rest here? I'm a bit tired."

We turn off the path into a grove and sit down on the grass. I open up a bottle, pour the juice into a cup, and offer it to him. I drink from my own bottle as well.

Such a procedure will work out nicely. I need only a second to slip the cyanide into his cup. I'll have any number of chances.

The plan seems to be foolproof, but I continue to go over it checking for any oversights. The important thing is to make him believe in Riichi Umetani. If I can do that, he'll follow me like a lamb into the quiet forests of Mt. Hiei. The holiday mood of the tourist area will help dispel any mistrust. Even if somebody sees us, we won't arouse any suspicion.

All I have to do now is wait for him to come from Kyushu.

IN THE WORDS OF TEIZABURO ISHIOKA

An odd letter arrived from a complete stranger, one Umetani. It was sent by registered mail, and when I opened it I was surprised to find a money order for 4,000 yen enclosed.

I had an even bigger shock when I read the contents. The man says that he's a relative of Miyako. He thinks he's discovered the man who murdered her nine years ago, and he wants me to go to Kyoto and identify him. He must have heard somewhere that I had seen a man with Miyako on the train.

So it's been nine years, I thought. Time flies.

I had gone from Yawata back to my home village in Shimane Prefecture. Food was scarce in those days, so I had taken a holiday to enjoy some wholesome country cooking. That day I was returning from a visit to a friend in Tsuda. The train was jam-packed with people who'd been out trying to buy food in the countryside.

"Mr. Ishioka." A woman had called my name as I pushed my way through the crowd. It turned out to be Miyako, who worked at the Hatsuhana Bar in Yawata. Since I was a regular at the bar, I knew her well. She was sort of cute, with a round face; to tell the truth, I was interested in her myself.

Running into someone from Yawata around there was unexpected.

"Oh, Miyako? You're the last person I thought I'd see here. Where are you going?"

Miyako's tone was lively.

"To a hot spring. There's lots to buy in Shimane Prefecture, so I hope to pick up something good on the way back."

It seemed quite extravagant to come all this way just to go to a hot spring. Then I noticed a man sitting next to Miyako, looking out the window self-consciously and smoking a cigarette.

Humph. I realized that she was traveling with this guy. The peel of a mandarin orange lay at their feet, hinting at their intimacy. They must have shared an orange they had bought near Hagi.

I guess I was a little jealous, but I began to feel out of place. I wasn't in the mood for talking. When I got off at Hamada, I promised to drop by the bar when I got back to Yawata. Little did I know that I would never see Miyako again.

After I returned to Yawata, I'd stop by the Hatsuhana Bar from time to time, but Miyako was never there. I asked one of the other girls if she had quit.

"Why, honey, she's run away." I gave a start. "You had a crush on her, didn't you? My condolences. Without a word to anybody, she just upped and left. She'd been sleeping out a lot lately, so I figured she had hooked up with a good catch. Still, she had a lot of nerve to take off without even bothering to say goodbye. You want to know something strange. She left behind all her things. The boss says she's the type who'd have the cheek to show up even now, acting as if nothing had happened. But really, what a thing to do, and when we're so busy."

"I saw Miyako. She was with a guy on a Sanin Line train."

"You're kidding. When?" she asked excitedly.

I told her the details. The other girls came flocking over.

"Miyako went all the way out there, huh? I wonder where she ended up. Tell me what this guy looked like. Was he handsome?" one of the girls asked as she leaned over me.

I was at a loss for an answer. I knew I had looked at his face, and yet I couldn't recall it.

"Did he have a long or round face?"

"Hmm. Now which was it?"

"Did he wear glasses?"

"Hmm."

"Was he light-skinned, or dark like you?"

"Hmm."

"Oh, you're hopeless," the girls chided me.

A few months passed. One day, out of the blue, a policeman asked me to come down to the station to answer a few questions. What's this about, I wondered. It turned out that Miyako had been murdered.

"Miyako's decomposed body has been discovered in the forests of Shimane Prefecture. We found out who she was from what remained of her belongings; our theory is that she was murdered. You knew her when she worked at the Hatsuhana Bar, and we hear that you saw her on a Sanin Line train. Is that correct?" asked Chief Detective Tamura.

The Hatsuhana Bar girls must have blabbed, I thought. But I had no reason to hide anything, so I told him all I knew.

The chief listened carefully.

"When was this? Can you remember the date?"

"Let me see. I went back to the country on June fifteenth, and I believe it was three or four days later. That makes it around the eighteenth or nineteenth."

"Where did the train pass through?"

"I got on at a station called Tsuda and got off at Hamada. It was between those stops."

The detective by the chief's side said, "Hamada is eight stops before Yunotsu." The chief nodded.

"Everything matches. This clinches it." He exchanged glances with the other detectives and then turned his attention to me. "Was Miyako alone at the time?"

"No, there was a man I didn't know sitting next to her."

"Did they speak to each other?"

"No, but I could tell they were together from the orange peel lying at their feet. Also, while I was talking to Miyako, the man kept looking out the window in a self-conscious way. In such a situation that's just how a fellow acts with his girl."

"I see." The chief smiled.

"Tell me, can you remember what he looked like?"

As the police had established that this man was the murderer, this question was crucial to them.

However, it also put me in a real quandary. I had definitely looked at his face, but when I was asked to describe it, I couldn't, just like when the girls at the Hatsuhana Bar asked me. Even with the police, I just couldn't remember.

And yet how could I say I had no recollection? A vague image had to be somewhere in my memory. After all, I had seen him with my own eyes. He must have made some impression on me. But for some strange reason I couldn't bring it to mind.

"Can't you try to remember?" the detective asked repeatedly.

"I'm really not sure." I scratched my head. A detective brought in a stack of mug shots.

"Look these over," the chief said. "These are photographs of men with criminal records. Pick out the ones that seem to fit his face. This man has the same profile; this one has the same hairstyle; his forehead looked like this; his eyebrows are like this; his nose, his lips, his chin, and so on. As you go through these photos, it'll come back to you. Just relax and look carefully."

The chief was insistent.

I went over the mug shots one by one. Most of them struck me as completely different. There were some that seemed to resemble his profile, and others that brought to mind his eyebrows. But I couldn't trust my memory. In the end, the more I looked, the more confused I got. My head was spinning.

"I just can't remember. I'm sorry." I bowed, sweating nervously.

The detectives could barely hide their disappointment.

"Go home and give it some more thought. It might come back to you in your sleep tonight," said Chief Detective Tamura, who seemed unable to admit defeat. At last I was allowed to go home. Of course, when I slipped into my bedding that night, I did not recall a thing.

Still, the detectives kept on visiting me. "How is it going? Can you remember now?" they'd ask. But after a while they stopped coming so I guess they gave up hope. According to the newspaper, a thorough search had been conducted for Miyako's killer, but nothing came of it and the case was closed as an un-solved murder.

Now this letter. I would never have imagined that after nine years the incident would surface again in such a way. I'm to look at the face of the man he suspects, and I have to make a special trip all the way to Kyoto to do so.

Even back then I knew I couldn't remember what he looked like. So if I were to see his face after all this time, what chance was there that I'd be able to identify it?

I wondered what to do. The 4,000 yen money order weighed heavily on me. If only he hadn't sent the money, I could have ig-nored the letter. What's more, I didn't know his address. He wrote that he was traveling. So I could neither return the money nor write a reply. And the appointed day was drawing closer.

He said that he was a relative of Miyako. I didn't know how he had managed to unearth the suspect, but finding him after all this time must have been the will of Heaven. Now he needed some-one to clinch it, so he wanted me to confirm that it was the same face I had seen.

What a predicament. I didn't know how to handle it. As I had dealt with the police at the beginning, I felt the best thing to do was discuss the problem with them.

I went to see Chief Detective Tamura at the station and showed him the letter.

"Well, well." He read the letter repeatedly and also checked the postmark. It was from a Kyoto post office. Tamura had been in charge of the murder investigation at the time so naturally he was eager to pursue the matter. He took the letter with him into another room. It was obvious that he had gone to discuss it with one of his superiors. After about thirty minutes he returned, his face flushed with excitement.

"Mr. Ishioka, I want you to go to Kyoto."

He spoke forcefully, as though he was ordering me.

"I want you to do as the letter says."

"But, Inspector, I'm not at all confident that I'll be able to recall his face even if I see it."

"No, you can never tell. If you actually saw him, his face might come back to you. We'll see what happens. Anyway, I want you to go. Two of our detectives will accompany you."

"But it says in the letter not to contact the police beforehand."

"Don't worry. We have our own ideas. I want you to take a good look at the face of the man who wrote this letter. We'll make sure he doesn't spot the detectives."

"What?" I had a shock. "Are you saying that you suspect Riichi Umetani?"

"Mr. Ishioka." Tamura bent toward me over his desk and lowered his voice. "Until a case is solved, no one is above suspicion. We believe that this man called Riichi Umetani is a fake. Can you see why? The person who wrote this letter knew that you had seen a man traveling with Miyako on the train. This was reported in the papers at the time, but your name was not revealed. Somewhere he learned that it was you."

"What?"

"For a start, the girls at the Hatsuhana Bar knew it was you and they might have passed on the information to someone else. But how about you?"

"I didn't tell anyone besides the bar girls. From the start you warned me not to say anything."

"In which case, that narrows it down to whoever the girls might have spoken to. An area, let's say, within Yawata City, or at most the Kita-Kyushu region. It's possible that somebody in this area might have heard about it. However, they wouldn't be likely to know your full name and correct address. There'd be no need to mention it; and no need for them to ask. The Hatsuhana Bar girls probably referred to you simply as 'Mr. Ishioka, a regular here.' They wouldn't know more; and neither would it make any difference to anyone. Yet the person who wrote this letter found out your exact name and address. Where could he have obtained this? Considering he's from Nagoya, he's knows rather a lot, doesn't he? In other words, he wrote the letter forgetting that the information he had personally sought out was not common knowledge. Look, as proof of his special interest in you, isn't the address on the envelope your current address, not where you lived at the time of the murder? That's quite a feat. Even grant-

54

ing that he had somehow gotten hold of your address at the time, wouldn't he have sent the letter to your former address? In that case the post office would have forwarded the letter. And yet the fact that he has your current address means that he was even aware that you had moved. And he carelessly wrote down everything he knew. Doesn't this prove that Riichi Umetani has been keeping tabs on you? For what reason, I don't know. But we want to find out who he is. That's why you've got to go to Kyoto." Tamura had spoken without a pause.

While I was listening, I began to feel a little uneasy, so I agreed. All this just because I had seen Miyako on the train nine years ago.

In order to fulfill the letter's stipulation that we meet in Kyoto Station at 2:30 P.M. on April 2, two detectives and I boarded an express train at Orio Station the night of April 1. The "Genkai" express left at 9:43 P.M..

Neither I nor the two detectives had been to Kyoto before. We all felt somewhat excited, in spite of the tension.

I didn't sleep well on the train. Finally, I dozed off around dawn. The two detectives sitting in front of me had fallen asleep without any trouble. I woke up suddenly to bright morning light streaming in from the windows. The detectives were enjoying a smoke.

"Had a good sleep, did you?"

"I guess so."

I went to wash, shaving kit in hand, and when I got back to my seat, the sun had completely risen.

The train was running along the coast. The ocean sparkled calmly in the morning light, and while distant Awaji Island glided slowly past, the pine forests outside the window whipped by at full speed.

"So that's the coast of Suma."

The detective gazed at the famous view untiringly.

As I looked at him, I felt I had seen the same scene somewhere before. It wasn't the detective himself so much as his pose, which I vaguely felt I had seen in a dream once. Every so often I experience this sort of déjà-vu. I might imagine I've already been to a place I've never visited. Or, for example, when I'm talking to somebody while walking down a lonely road, I might feel that I had dreamed that exact scene. It's an unnerving quirk.

We arrived at Kyoto Station at 10:19. There was plenty of time before the 2:30 appointment. Since we had had breakfast on the train, we decided to go sightseeing. After all, we had come all the way to Kyoto.

We started with Higashi Hongan Temple near the station, went on to Sanjusangen-do and Kiyomizu temples, and then walked around downtown. One of the detectives took out his watch. "It's noon. How about getting something to eat before heading back to the station?"

"Good idea. Let's eat one of the local specialties—I'd like to try *imobo*," said the other.

"*Imobo*? Sounds expensive."

"What does it matter? Either way we're bound to exceed our budget for the trip. We may never have the chance to come back to Kyoto, so why not?"

The matter settled, we headed for a restaurant next to Gion's Maruyama Park.

"Are there three of you?" the waitress asked. "I'm sorry, all the rooms are full. But if you don't mind sharing . . ."

We said we didn't and were led into a six-mat room.

There was a man there eating by himself. . . .

FROM THE DIARY OF RYOKICHI INO

April 2. The day has finally come.

Last night I took the "Gekko" train from Tokyo, and after reaching Kyoto in the morning I found I had six full hours to kill. With nothing better to do, I visited the Temple of the Golden Pavilion and toured Mt. Arashi.

The weather was good. At Mt. Arashi, the buds on the cherry trees were already taking on color. I crossed over Togetsu Bridge, came back, and took a taxi to Shijo Avenue; it was 11:30.

I was a little hungry. What should I eat? Since I had come to Kyoto, I wanted something I couldn't get in Tokyo. I settled for *imobo*.

I got off the tram car at Yasaka Shrine and walked toward Maruyama Park. It was the season for school trips and group tours from the countryside, so the area was fairly crowded with sightseers.

I was served the specialty in a private room. As I ate, I thought of my confrontation with Ishioka that was to take place two hours later. I was about to take a gamble that would decide my fate. I had to survive by whatever means possible; I had to win. In anyone's life, there comes a time when happiness smiles on you. Either you make a grab for it or you let it get away—in this way is success or ruin determined. And I wanted to succeed.

It was my mistake to have gotten involved with a worthless female like Miyako. But if I had let such a woman dig her claws into me, I'd never have amounted to anything. She had used her pregnancy to bind me to her. Even when I had insisted she have an abortion, she had refused point-blank, her face pale and menacing. She had desperately tried to make me succumb to her will. And I had done everything in my power to escape. The thought of the gloomy, miserable life we'd have together had been more than I could bear. If I had ended up in such a predicament, I might have gone crazy. I knew then that I had to murder her.

Even now I don't regret anything. And yet I may lose all my good fortune just because I killed a worthless woman. What could be more ludicrous?

If I had killed a real beauty, a truly valuable woman, I would have willingly offered my life in exchange. But how could I justify giving up my happiness to compensate for Miyako, who to me was the stupidest, ugliest woman in the world?

All the same, it is bad luck for Ishioka that my success depends on having my face seen in movies. In order for this one man never to see my face, I have to shut his eyes permanently. No matter what it takes, I want to live. I want fame and money. I want the good life.

Just then, the waitress came in and I looked up. She asked if I minded sharing the room with three other customers. I consented. The three customers entered. I continued eating.

"Excuse me." One of them apologized as he sat down at a separate table right across from me.

A couple of feet away, two of the guests were facing each other on my right and left, while the third was sitting directly opposite me. The waitress brought them hot towels. They were talking as they wiped their faces.

They were speaking with a Kyushu accent. I looked up, startled. My eyes focused directly on the man wiping his face in front of me.

My heart stopped.

I couldn't breathe.

I was frozen to the spot, unable to turn my gaze away. If I forced myself to look away, I was sure something horrible would happen.

The man right in front of me. The heavy eyebrows, the bulging eyes—the man of nine years ago, Teizaburo Ishioka!

An inane scream welled up inside of me. How could this be happening? How could the man I arranged to meet at Kyoto Station at 2:30 be sitting here?

I felt the blood drain from my face. What should I do? I wasn't wearing any makeup. Neither did I have my hat or spectacles. My face was fully exposed to him, just as it was that time. There was no way to escape. What should I do? Who were his companions? My ears were ringing. The surroundings suddenly grew dim. I felt as if I were sinking.

Ishioka quietly looked in my direction.

Not able to wait for his shout, I felt an urge to let out a cry myself. My body quivered violently. The fingers holding my chopsticks had gone numb.

The lacquered chopsticks I was holding made a small sound as they fell onto the tatami mats. But his gentle expression didn't change. He was listening to his two companions. Occasionally he would make a reply. He had an unassuming presence. Perhaps it was the passage of nine years, but he seemed to have aged quite a bit.

This lasted for thirty seconds. Then one minute. Nothing happened. They were talking in low voices, but there was no change in their tone.

The waitress brought their lunch. The three immediately started to eat. Ishioka looked down. His attention was concentrated on the local specialty.

What could this mean? He had just looked at my face. And yet he hadn't registered the slightest reaction. Had he forgotten what I looked like perhaps? Then I suddenly understood.

What a joke! From the very beginning he hadn't remembered my face. I had only left a vague impression on him. He hadn't looked at my face closely.

Of course. That was it.

Suddenly I felt as if I was being gently lifted up to heaven. What a thing to happen!

I took a deep breath. Then I stood up. I slowly crossed the tatami-mat floor while reaching in my pocket for a cigarette. An extraordinary surge of confidence welled up inside me.

I had figured out everything. Having received the 4,000 yen, the conscientious Ishioka felt compelled to come to Kyoto. When he met the man in the cap and glasses, he would scratch his head and apologize: "I'm sorry. I can't remember him very well." He was an honest, good-natured fellow. The other two were probably his friends. They had most likely come along to go sightseeing in Kyoto.

I was completely calm. I called out to them. It was a bold experiment.

"I'd like to smoke. Do you have a match?"

Ishioka suddenly looked up at me. I felt my features stiffen in spite of myself. He silently handed me the matches on the table.

"Thanks." I lit up. Ishioka, having taken no special notice of me, returned to gobbling down the *imobo*.

I left the restaurant. Maruyama Park had never looked so beautiful. The Kyoto scenery had never seemed so soothing.

Goodbye to the waiting room at Kyoto Station and Mt. Hiei.

I laughed aloud to myself. And while laughing, my tears began to flow.

IN THE WORDS OF TEIZABURO ISHIOKA

No matter how long we waited at Kyoto Station, a man fitting that description never appeared. Two-thirty had long since passed. Four o'clock came. Five o'clock.

At eight o'clock, we decided he wasn't coming.

The two detectives were disappointed. Was it a practical joke? But why send 4,000 yen just for a joke? The detectives were convinced that it was serious. They told me that he might have caught on to us.

Caught on? But how?

One part of me was unable to calm down somehow.

We discussed whether it was worth waiting one more day, just in case, but concluded that it would be pointless. We returned to Kyushu that evening by the night express train.

It was a strange two days.

FROM THE DIARY OF RYOKICHI INO

Filming for *The Red Forest* is progressing smoothly.

I had no idea that peace of mind could make such a difference. My entire body is alive with confidence.

I can do it!

***

We're almost finished shooting. My part is over, so I can relax a bit.

This director also seems to be quite taken with me. He told me that he's looking for an unusual script in which he can use me for the lead. I'm on my way up.

***

The Red Forest has been released. The newspaper reviews have been favorable. They have all praised "Ryokichi Ino's excellent and original performance."

Y. was overjoyed.

***

Today I had offers from two other film companies. I'm leaving everything to Y., which seems wisest for the time being.

It's all turning out just as I wanted. Fame and money are well within my reach. I recited my favorite passage to myself: "After I made a lot of money, I didn't know how to spend it. I thought of hiding myself in a private room in a huge, fancy restaurant, sipping champagne and hiring my own gypsy to play for me. And I would listen to the music and sob."

IN THE WORDS OF TEIZABURO ISHIOKA

It'd been a long time since I'd gone to a movie. *The Red Forest* was playing. I heard that it had gotten good reviews in the papers. It was a sort of serious film with almost no action—what's called an art film, I guess.

An unknown actor by the name of Ryokichi Ino (New Wave, it seems) had a prominent role. The character he played went to visit a married woman at her villa in Hakone. The story unfolded against the backdrop of the Hakone mountains. Ino, broken-hearted, descended the mountain and boarded a train at Odawara. He was looking out the window. The scenery around Oiso flowed by. He took out a cigarette and smoked, still looking out the window.

The scenery changed to somewhere near Chigasaki.

Ino's face looking out the window. Smoking a cigarette. The scenery around Totsuka.

Ino's profile as he looked out the window! . . . I had a shock. I had seen it before somewhere.

It wasn't a dream. It was a long time ago, but it had definitely happened. I had felt the same way when I saw the detective in the Kyoto-bound train.

A close-up of Ino's face. His profile as he stared out the window. Wisps of smoke from the cigarette floated up, making his eyes smart. His eyes half-closed and his brow furrowed. That expression! His face!

I was seized by a horrible realization. Unwittingly I let out a cry. Those around me turned in their seats in surprise.

I dashed out of the movie theater. Despite my thumping heart, I made off as fast as I could to the police station. I had to tell someone about my suspicions as soon as possible.

The Serial

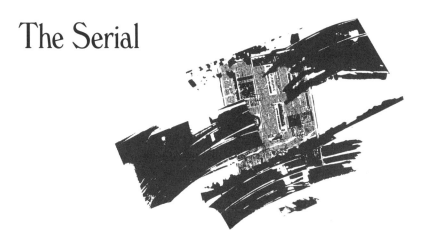

1

Yoshiko Shioda sent in a subscription for the *Koshin News*. The newspaper office was located in K., a city about two and a half hours away from Tokyo by express train. The paper seemed quite influential in the prefecture, but, of course, it was not available at Tokyo newsstands. If you wanted to read it in Tokyo, you had no choice but to subscribe directly.

On February 21 she sent the payment by registered mail. Along with the money, she enclosed the following letter:

"I would like to subscribe to your newspaper, and I am enclosing payment for the subscription. The novel *The Romance of the Country Bandit*, which is being serialized in your paper, looks very interesting, and I'd like to read it. Please send me the issues beginning from the nineteenth."

Yoshiko had seen a copy of the *Koshin News* when she had been in a dreary restaurant in front of K. Station. While she was waiting for her order of Chinese noodles to arrive, the waitress had placed a copy on the rough-hewn table top. The crude printing was typical of a provincial paper. The third page was given over to local news: a fire had destroyed five houses; an official from the town office had embezzled 60,000 yen from public funds; construction had been completed on the elementary school annex; the mother of a prefectural congressman had died—this kind of article.

At the bottom of page two there was a serialized historical novel. The illustration depicted two samurai locked in battle. She had never heard of the author, one Ryuji Sugimoto. When her noodles arrived, she stopped reading it halfway, but she jotted down the name and address of the paper in her notebook. She also made a mental note of the novel's title, *The Romance of the Country Bandit*. "Chapter 54" was written beneath the title. The date was February 18.

There were still seven minutes to go before three o'clock. Yoshiko left the restaurant and walked around. The town nestled in a valley, and an unusually warm winter sunlight filled the clear highland sky. To the south a chain of mountains rose gently, and behind them the upper half of a snow-white Mt. Fuji was visible. In the strong light Mt. Fuji seemed strangely out of focus.

Straight ahead was the snow-covered Mt. Kaikomagadake. The sun was hitting the snow at an angle, so that the folds in the mountain created alternating patches of light and darkness. To the right of this mountain, and closer, lay a chain of smaller mountains, the color of brown leaves. She couldn't see into their valleys. But something was about to happen there. For Yoshiko, these mountains had a special significance.

Yoshiko returned to the station square. A large crowd of people had gathered there, and over the darkish heads fluttered some white banners, on which were written the words, "Welcome Home, Minister M." A month earlier a new cabinet had been formed, and Yoshiko had heard that one of the ministers was from these parts.

Before long the crowd started to stir excitedly. Some people shouted "*Banzai!*" There was loud clapping. Passersby ran to join the fringe of the gathering.

There was a speech. The minister addressed the crowd from a platform, with the winter sun shining on his bald head. On his chest was a large white rosette. The crowd listened in silence punctuated by occasional bursts of applause.

Yoshiko was watching the people. And she wasn't the only one. A man standing next to her was also gazing at the scene. He wasn't listening to the speech but appeared to be standing there reluctantly since his way was blocked by the crowd.

Yoshiko stole a glance at his profile. A wide forehead, piercing eyes, a straight nose. She had once thought the forehead intelligent, the eyes honest, and the nose attractive. It was an empty memory now, but he still had the power to mesmerize her.

The speech finally came to an end and the minister stepped down from the dais. Gaps appeared as the crowd began to break up. Yoshiko started walking. So did the man who had been standing next to her—and one other person. . . .

She made it to the post office near her apartment just before closing time at three, and sent her registered letter off to the *Koshin News.* She put her receipt in the bottom of her handbag and boarded a train from Chitose Karasuyama. The bar in Shibuya where she worked was fifty minutes away.

The neon sign read "Bar Rubicon." Yoshiko entered through the back. She greeted the manager, the other hostesses, and the waiters, then hurried to the dressing room to put on her makeup.

The bar was showing signs of life. When the fat proprietress arrived, just back from the beauty parlor, everyone was quick to praise her new hairdo.

"Today is Saturday, the twenty-first. I want you all to work hard."

Then the manager gave a pep-talk to the hostesses. Conscious of the presence of the proprietress, he told A. to get a new dress, which embarrassed her no end.

As Yoshiko listened absentmindedly, the thought occurred to her that it was time to quit here as well.

In her mind she saw a ship cutting through the waves. Over the last few days this image was so persistent it wouldn't leave her, day or night. When she pressed her hand to her heart, she could feel painful palpitations.

2

The *Koshin News* arrived four or five days later. They sent several days' worth all at once. Also enclosed was a printed postcard thanking her for the subscription.

The papers were from the nineteenth, as she had requested. She opened up the first one and turned to the page of local news: somebody's house had been robbed; someone had died in a landslide; there were irregularities in the farmers' union accounts; the campaign for the town council had begun—nothing of any interest. There was also a big photograph of Minister M. in front of K. Station.

Yoshiko opened the paper dated the twentieth. There was nothing special. She looked at the one dated the twenty-first. Here, too, there were only ordinary articles. She threw the papers into the corner of her closet. She could use them as wrapping paper or something.

From then on the newspaper was delivered daily. As Yoshiko was a regular subscriber, her name and address had been mimeographed on the brown wrapper. Every morning she'd go to her mailbox to get it. She'd tear off the wrapper in bed—since she got home around midnight, she'd always sleep in—spread the paper out over her quilt and look at it carefully from the first page to the last. There'd be nothing that particularly attracted her interest. She would then fling the paper aside in disgust.

This continued for a number of days. And each time she experienced the same disappointment. But until she ripped off the brown wrapper, she always had hope. This "hope" also persisted day after day. But as always, there was never anything different.

Finally, there *was* something different on the fifteenth day— that is, when the paper had arrived for the fifteenth time. It wasn't an article but an unexpected postcard from a Ryuji Sugimoto. The name seemed vaguely familiar. She couldn't recall where, but she knew she had seen it before.

Yoshiko turned the card over. The handwriting was atrocious. As soon as she read it she remembered.

"I would like to express my appreciation for the interest you have shown in my novel *The Romance of the Country Bandit*, which is being serialized in the *Koshin News*. I look forward to your continued support."

Ryuji Sugimoto was the author of the serial carried in the newspaper that came in the brown paper wrapper. Someone from the newspaper office must have informed him that Yoshiko had subscribed to the paper because she wanted to read his novel. Sugimoto must have been so pleased that he decided to write this thank-you note to his new fan.

It was a small variation. But it was different from the one she had been expecting. An extraneous postcard had intruded itself. She had no intention of reading his novel. In any event, it was sure to be as bad as the handwriting on the postcard.

The paper came regularly every day. This was only to be expected since she had paid for it. And Yoshiko did not fail to go through it in bed every morning. But there was never anything in it. How long would this disappointment continue, she wondered.

It happened on a morning almost one month after she had subscribed to the paper. As always, the page was a hodgepodge of poorly printed local news: the head of the farmers' union had run off; a bus had slipped off a cliff, causing injuries; a mountain fire had razed two acres; the bodies of two lovers who had committed suicide had been discovered in Rinun Gorge.

Yoshiko read the article about the suicides. Their bodies had been found in the forests of Rinun Gorge by an inspector from the forestry office. A month had passed since their deaths, so the decomposed corpses were almost skeletons. Their identities were unknown. There was nothing unusual about the incident. This isolated ravine with its strangely shaped rocks and sparkling streams was a well-known spot for lovers' suicides.

Yoshiko folded the paper, lay back on her pillow, and pulled the quilt up to her chin. She stared at the ceiling. It was an old apartment house and the boards on the grimy ceiling were starting to rot. Yoshiko continued to stare blankly.

The next morning's paper seemed duty-bound to report the identities of the bodies. The man was thirty-five and had worked as a security guard at a Tokyo department store; the woman was twenty-two and had been employed at the same store. The man had a wife and child. It was something that happened all the time. Yoshiko looked up. She was without feeling—a kind of emotionless peace of mind. The paper no longer interested her. Once more, she had a sharp vision of the ship racing through the ocean.

Two or three days later a postcard came from the sales department of the *Koshin News*.

"Your subscription has run out. We look forward to your continued readership." How efficient of them!

Yoshiko wrote a reply: "The novel has gotten boring. I do not wish to renew my subscription."

She mailed the postcard on her way to work. After she had dropped it in the postbox, it occurred to her that the author of *The Romance of the Country Bandit* would probably take it badly. I shouldn't have written that, she reproached herself.

3

When Ryuji Sugimoto read the postcard the *Koshin News* had forwarded to him, his mood turned sour. It was from the same woman who, only a month earlier, had subscribed to the paper because she had found his novel interesting. That time the newspaper had also forwarded her letter. He had even sent her a brief thank-you note. Now she wrote that she was cancelling her subscription because the novel had gotten boring.

"Women are such fickle fans," Ryuji thought angrily.

The Romance of the Country Bandit had been commissioned by a literary agency that specialized in serials for local papers. Although he had tailored his novel to meet the standards of such popular fiction, he had taken the work seriously. It was by no means a slap-dash effort and he was confident of its appeal. That was why he had been so happy to hear that a Tokyo resident had gone out of her way to read his novel, and had even written her that note to thank her for her interest.

And now this very reader had cancelled her subscription

because she found the novel boring. Ryuji gave a cynical laugh, but anger was welling up inside him. He felt he had been made a fool of. Then he began to wonder. She had canceled her subscription just when the story was really getting interesting—much more so than the part she said she had liked. There were exciting developments in the plot, and lively action scenes were coming fast and furious. He himself was delighted with the novel's progress.

"How could she say it's gotten boring?" he asked himself. Since he was confident of his ability to please his public, such a capricious reader upset him no end.

Ryuji was by no means famous, but he was a regular contributor to magazines and had a reputation as a skillful writer. For some time he had flattered himself that he had mastered the art of giving the public what it wanted. The novel currently being serialized in the *Koshin News* was definitely not of inferior quality. He was writing in top form.

"My mood's shot."

Two days later he still couldn't get rid of the bad aftertaste. By the third day he started to feel better, but inside him a bitter residue remained. Each day this feeling would surface now and again. It was worse than having a work that he had labored over criticized unfairly by some pro. What disturbed him was the undeniable fact that the newspaper had lost a sale as a result of his novel. To exaggerate a bit, he felt as if he had lost face with the newspaper.

Ryuji shook his head and got up from his desk to go for a walk. He went along a path he always took, through an area where the scent of the Musashi plains still lingered. On the far side of a grove strewn with fallen leaves a pond sparkled in the winter sun.

He sat down on the withered grass and looked at the water. By the side of the pond a foreigner was training a large dog. The dog would dash off to retrieve a stick thrown for it, and then run back to its owner. This was repeated over and over again.

He gazed at them impersonally. When one looks at monotonous, repetitive action, an unexpected thought can pop into one's head. Suddenly a certain doubt began to trouble Ryuji.

"She started reading my novel from the middle. She said that it was interesting, but where had she heard of it?"

The *Koshin News* was only sold in that prefecture. It was not available in Tokyo, so obviously there was no way she could have known about it there. Which means that this Tokyo woman who called herself Yoshiko Shioda had either lived somewhere in the prefecture or had seen the paper when she came on a visit from Tokyo.

Lost in thought, his eyes mechanically followed the dog's movements. Even if this was the case, a woman who had been so drawn to his novel that she would go out of her way to subscribe to it directly from the newspaper office wasn't very likely to lose interest so quickly and cancel her subscription within a month. Especially when the novel itself had actually gotten more interesting.

Something's fishy, he thought. She can't have subscribed to the newspaper to read my novel. That was some excuse she thought up. The truth is that she was interested in something else. In other words, she was searching for something in the paper. And once she found it, she no longer had any need of the paper.

Ryuji got up off the grass and hurried home. These thoughts in his head were churning around like a bunch of seaweed tugged this way and that by the current.

Once home, he took out from his file the first letter from Yoshiko that the newspaper had forwarded.

"I would like to subscribe to your newspaper, and I am enclosing payment for the subscription. The novel *The Romance of the Country Bandit*, which is being serialized in your paper, looks very interesting, and I'd like to read it. Please send me the issues beginning from the nineteenth."

Her handwriting was rather precise for a woman. More curiously, why did she specifically ask that the subscription be predated two days before she wrote the letter, to start from the nineteenth? At the fastest, newspaper articles can only report the events of the day before, and the *Koshin News* had no evening edition. If she wanted to read the paper from the nineteenth, it

70

meant that she wanted to learn of something that had occurred on the eighteenth or after, he concluded.

He had been getting the paper daily. Opening up the file on his desk, he looked carefully through each back issue, starting with the one of the nineteenth. He paid special attention to the local news, but, just to be certain, he also looked over the advertisements and want ads.

He was limiting his search to articles that linked the prefecture to Tokyo. With that in mind, he read through each day's news. There was nothing suitable on any day in February. He started on March. There was nothing up to the fifth. Nothing through the tenth. The thirteenth, the fourteenth. Finally, in the paper dated the sixteenth, he hit upon the following article.

"On March 15, around 2 P.M., an inspector from the forestry office discovered two corpses from a lovers' suicide in the forests of Rinun Gorge. As the bodies were badly decomposed, almost skeletons, approximately a month is thought to have passed since death. The man had been wearing a gray overcoat and a navy blue suit. His age is estimated at thirty-seven. The woman had been wearing a brown coat with large checks and a suit of the same color; her age was approximately twenty-two. The only article left on the scene was the woman's handbag containing her makeup. Inside was a round-trip ticket from Shinjuku to K. Station, which seems to indicate that the couple was from Tokyo. . . ."

There was another article the next day.

"The identities of the victims of the lovers' suicide at Rinun Gorge have been established—Sakiji Shoda (35), a security guard at a Tokyo department store, and Umeko Fukuda (22), an employee at the same store. The man was married and had a child. Police are treating it as a case of suicide due to a hopeless love affair."

"That's it."

Ryuji had inadvertently let out a shout. Here was the link between Tokyo and the prefecture. Yoshiko must have cancelled her subscription after the appearance of this article, which would never appear in the Tokyo papers. That must be the reason why she had gone out of her way to subscribe to the local paper.

"Wait a minute." Another thought occurred to him.

Yoshiko had started her subscription from February 19. The bodies were discovered on March 15, approximately one month after death. In that case, the suicides would have occurred before the nineteenth. The time matches! She knew of the suicides! She was waiting for the bodies to be discovered. Why?

Ryuji suddenly became extremely interested in the woman called Yoshiko Shioda. He stared at her address.

4

Three weeks later a reply came from the private detective Ryuji had hired.

Findings of the Investigation Requested on Yoshiko Shioda

Yoshiko Shioda comes from S. Village in T. County, H. Prefecture. Her present address is Shinkuso Apartments, 1 Karasuyama-cho, Setagaya Ward. According to the copy of her family register, she is married to one Hayao Shioda. The superintendent of her apartment house described her as a quiet person who rented the apartment on her own three years ago. She recently told him that her husband, who was in a Russian prisoner-of-war camp, would be coming home soon. She works as a hostess in the Rubicon Bar in Shibuya.

According to the bar proprietress, Yoshiko has been working there for a year; previously she was employed at the Angel Bar in West Ginza. The proprietress described her as ladylike. Although she has a number of regular customers, she doesn't seem to be going out with anyone in particular. But there was one man—thin, around thirty-five—who'd come two or three times a month and specifically ask for her. As she always paid his bill, the proprietress concluded that they must have been involved in a serious way during her days at the Angel Bar. The two of them would always sit alone in a booth and talk in low voices. Once, when one of the other hostesses asked if he was her boyfriend, Yoshiko had made a face. Whenever he came to the bar she looked depressed. No one knew his name.

Inquiries at the Angel Bar confirmed that Yoshiko had indeed worked there until a year ago and had had a good reputation. But she hadn't been a very outgoing hostess and had never attracted a lot of customers. A man fitting the description given at the Rubicon had visited her here as well, although he only started showing up about three months before she quit. In other words, she had changed her place of work to the Rubicon three months after his first visit.

Next, concerning your request for information on Mr. Sakiji Shoda, the security guard at T. Department Store, his wife did not have one good word to say about him. His suicide with another woman seems to have made her bitter. She said that although his job at the department store was watching out for shoplifters and thieves, he had no better morals himself and spent most of his money on his love affairs. His wife was aware that Umeko Fukuda, who had worked at the same department store, committed suicide with him. "He's brought me nothing but disgrace," she exclaimed indignantly.

She even said that she refused to place her husband's urn on the household altar, and that she had tied it up with string and shoved it in the closet. When we asked her about Yoshiko, she replied, "I don't know any such woman. But he was a downright lecher and I never knew what he was doing." We calmed her down and succeeded in borrowing a photograph of her husband.

When we showed the photo to the owners and hostesses at the Rubicon and Angel bars, they all said that it was definitely the man who had visited Yoshiko.

We returned to her apartment house and showed the photo to the superintendent. He looked embarrassed, and said, "Actually, I didn't want to bring this kind of thing up, but he'd come to visit her three or four times a month. He'd often stay two nights."

This confirms that Yoshiko Shioda and Sakiji Shoda were lovers. But how they met is still unclear.

As requested, we asked the superintendent about her movements on February 18. He can't remember the exact day, but around then she definitely left her apartment at ten or so in the morning. He remembered it because she usually slept in late.

According to the Rubicon's roster, Yoshiko had a day off on February 18.

This concludes our investigations so far. Please let us know if you would like us to pursue any specific point further.

Ryuji read the report over twice.

Professionals really know how to do their job, he thought. Quite a thorough investigation.

In this way it was established that Yoshiko was clearly involved in Sakiji's and Umeko's double suicide. There was no doubt that she had known the two had killed themselves in Rinun Gorge. On February 18, the day of the suicide, she had gotten up early and taken the day off work. Rinun Gorge was near K. Station on the Chuo Line. Where had she seen them off? At Shinjuku? At K. Station?

He looked at a train schedule. Chuo Line express trains from Shinjuku heading for K. City left at 8:10 and 12:25. The night train was out of the question. And he could more or less eliminate local trains. If she had gone to K. Station, she would surely have taken an express.

Assuming Yoshiko had left her apartment around ten o'clock, she could have caught the local train at 11:32, but it was more likely she would have taken the 12:25 express. She would have arrived at K. Station at 3:05 P.M. From the station to where the suicide occurred in Rinun Gorge would have taken a full hour by bus and on foot. Which meant that Sakiji and Umeko would have arrived at the scene of their suicide just as the winter sun was about to set. Ryuji pictured the couple wandering through the forests of the mountain ravine with its jagged rocks.

For about a month, until an inspector from the forestry office discovered the decomposed bodies, Yoshiko was the only one who knew about them. She had been reading the local paper to find out when the event became public knowledge. Just where did she fit in?

Once more he looked through the *Koshin News* dated February 19. A landslide; irregularities in the farmers' union; elections for the town council—nothing out of the ordinary. There was a big photograph of Minister M., a native of the area, giving a speech in front of K. Station.

His eyes were drawn to the photograph. Just as when he had gazed at the monotonous, repetitive movements of the dog, ideas began to fill his head. Although his deadline was only a day away, Ryuji laid aside his manuscript and brooded, his head in his hands. He would never have believed that the loss of one reader could have affected him so.

His wife would undoubtedly have assumed he was struggling with his novel.

5

Yoshiko, along with four or five other hostesses, was attending to a customer when she was told that somebody had asked for her. A long-haired, plumpish man in his early forties was sitting alone in a booth. Yoshiko had no idea who he was. It was his first visit to the Rubicon Bar.

"Are you Yoshiko? Yoshiko Shioda?" the man asked, smiling.

Yoshiko went by her own first name at the bar, but when he called her by her full name, she was startled and looked at him more closely. The lighting was dim, but there was a lamp with a pink shade on the table. The face that floated in its red glow was completely unfamiliar.

"That's correct. Who are you?" She sat down by his side.

The man reached in his pocket and handed her a name card, soiled around the edges. When she brought it to the light she could make out the letters RYUJI SUGIMOTO. Her heart skipped a beat.

"That's right. I'm the author of *The Romance of the Country Bandit*, which you've been kind enough to read." Ryuji's face had broken into a wide grin. "My thanks. I heard of you from the *Koshin News*. And I believe I sent you a note. Actually, as I was in your neighborhood yesterday, I took the liberty of dropping by your apartment, but you weren't home. I was told that you work here, so I decided to surprise you tonight. I wanted to thank you in person."

Yoshiko was taken aback. Had he really gone to these lengths just because she had praised his novel? She had never even seriously read *The Romance of the Country Bandit*. Some novelists were awfully easy to please.

"Why, it's you. And to have come all this way! I find your novel fascinating." She edged closer to him and smiled affably.

"Thanks." Ryuji seemed even more pleased as he gazed around him diffidently. "It's a nice place." He looked shyly at Yoshiko. "And you're quite beautiful," he added in a whisper.

"Oh, come on now. I'm delighted to meet you. And I don't want you rushing off." As she poured his beer, she looked at him coquettishly and smiled. Does he still think I'm reading his novel, she wondered. He can't be very popular if he gets so excited over one fan. Or maybe his interest was sparked by the fact that I'm a woman.

Ryuji, it turned out, was not a drinker. One bottle of beer had turned his face bright red. But Yoshiko and several other hostesses who flocked over were also drinking, so the table was covered with a colorful assortment of bottles and dishes. As the women kept flattering him, Ryuji seemed to be enjoying himself immensely. He left about an hour later.

Just after he had gone, Yoshiko noticed that a brown envelope had fallen behind his cushion. "It must be his," she exclaimed as she ran to the door. But he was nowhere in sight.

"He's sure to come again, so I'll keep it for him," she said to the hostess next to her. She tucked the envelope inside her kimono and forgot about it. She only remembered it again after she had returned home and had undone her obi. The brown envelope fell onto the tatami mats.

She picked it up. Nothing was written on either side of the unsealed envelope. She could see what looked like newsprint inside. In that case there's nothing wrong in taking a peek, she decided, her curiosity aroused.

A folded newspaper clipping about a quarter of a page in size lay before her. Yoshiko opened it. Her eyes widened. It was unmistakably a clipping from the *Koshin News*, a photo of Minister M. giving a speech in front of K. Station.

Above the pitch-black crowd several white flags were flutter-ing. The minister's figure rose above the crowd. It was a scene that Yoshiko had once gazed at with her own eyes. The photograph showed exactly the same scene.

Yoshiko stared into space. Her fingers were trembling slightly. Her loosened kimono hung open at her breast.

Was it coincidence, or had Ryuji deliberately left it behind to show to her? Confused, she sat down on the tatami, her legs giv-ing way. She didn't even have the energy to take out her bedding. Ryuji must know something. He had some reason in leaving the envelope, her intuition told her. It was definitely no coincidence.

Ryuji Sugimoto, who had seemed like a good-natured hack novelist, suddenly began to take on a new and sinister light in Yoshiko's eyes.

Two days later Ryuji put in another appearance at the bar. He asked for Yoshiko.

"Good evening." She gave a professional smile as she sat down next to him, but it seemed forced.

Ryuji returned her smile, his expression as guileless as before.

"You forgot this the other day." Yoshiko got up, took the brown envelope from her handbag, and handed it to him. Her lips held the smile, but her eyes were scrutinizing his face.

"I left it here then? I was wondering where I'd dropped it. Thank you."

He put the envelope in his pocket. He kept on grinning, but as he gazed at Yoshiko, his tiny eyes seemed to sparkle viciously for a moment. In the next instant he shifted his attention to his glass of foaming beer. Yoshiko could stand it no longer. She decided to try something. She knew it was dangerous, but she couldn't stop herself from making the experiment.

"What is it? Something important?"

"It's a photograph from a newspaper. A photo of a minister giv-ing a speech in K. City," Ryuji explained, revealing a row of white teeth. "There's a face in the crowd that bothers me. It's someone I knew, someone who committed suicide with his lover at Rinun Gorge."

"Oh my," exclaimed two other hostesses at the table.

"Right next to him are two women who seem to be with him. You see, they're all standing a bit away from the crowd. I have reason to believe that this was the day he and his lover committed suicide. In which case, it stands to reason that there'd be one woman with him. But why the third party? It's a little fishy. I'd like a better look at the faces of those two women, but the picture is too small to make them out. So I'm thinking of sending the clipping to the newspaper office and having them make an enlargement from the negative. It's just curiosity, but I want to look into it further."

"My goodness, you're like a detective."

The two hostesses laughed in unison. Yoshiko felt she was suffocating.

6

It was then that Yoshiko figured out Ryuji's real intentions.

He was lying. There were no faces in the photograph such as the ones he described. She knew because she herself had looked over the photo carefully. Neither Sakiji, Umeko, or herself appeared anywhere in the shot.

By claiming that something had been photographed that wasn't, Ryuji's intentions became clear to her. Obviously he had also lied about being a friend of Sakiji's. She was being put to a test. It might not be much of a threat in itself, but what frightened her was that he had started to get wind of something, and she was afraid of the consequences.

Ryuji's subsequent experiment, carried off casually enough, drove this fear home to her. One week later he showed up again at the bar. As always, he asked for Yoshiko.

"Remember the photograph I talked about the other day— well, it didn't work out," he said, smiling innocently. "The newspaper told me that they had thrown away the negative. It's too bad. It might have held an important clue."

"What a shame." Yoshiko drank her beer. She found his play-acting odious.

Then Ryuji's tone changed. "Lately I've taken up photography myself. I just got back some prints today. Do you want to see them?"

"Oh, I'd love to." One of the other girls came out with the expected flattering response.

"Here they are." He took out a few snaps from his pocket and placed them next to the plates on the table.

"Why, they're all pictures of the same couple," the hostess said as soon as she picked them up.

"That's right. The composition's quite good, isn't it?" Ryuji was grinning.

"You have weird tastes—taking pictures of some couple you don't know. Have a look at these, Yoshiko." She passed the photographs on.

From the moment Ryuji took the photographs out of his pocket, Yoshiko had had a premonition—a bad one. Apprehension made her tense up and shiver slightly. Her fears came true when she picked up the photographs and looked at them.

They were shots from the rear of a man and woman walking down a country road. It seemed to be the area around Musashi; the early spring forest cast shadows in both the foreground and background. Ordinary, everyday photographs. But what immediately caught Yoshiko's eyes was the couple's clothing. The man was wearing a light overcoat and dark trousers. On the woman's overcoat large checks were clearly visible. From the black-and-white photograph Yoshiko could conjure up a vivid image of Sakiji's gray overcoat and navy blue suit and the brown checkered coat and matching suit that Umeko had worn.

It's come at last, thought Yoshiko. As she had resigned herself, her heart wasn't beating all that quickly. When she looked down and stared at the photographs, all she could see was Ryuji's face. And she felt sparks flying as her gaze collided with his tiny, gleaming eyes.

"They're wonderful." She had to make a great effort to raise her head and casually return the photographs to their owner.

"Yes, they're rather good, aren't they?" he agreed as he stared at Yoshiko for a brief moment. His eyes were shining just the way

79

she had imagined while she was looking at the photographs.

Ryuji really had sniffed it out. He might figure out everything before long. A cold wind chilled her heart. That night she couldn't get to sleep until four in the morning.

Soon after that Yoshiko and Ryuji became more intimate. When he didn't appear at the bar, she phoned him to urge him to come. She'd also write him letters. These were different from the formal "business letters" hostesses normally wrote to bring customers in. Her letters were brimming with emotion.

In anyone's eyes, theirs was the relationship of a favored customer and his regular bar girl. Things between them had progressed extremely rapidly, considering how new he was at the bar. They had reached the stage where Yoshiko could make the following proposal to him.

"I'd love to go away with you somewhere. I can get the day off from work."

Ryuji smiled happily, his nose crinkling. "Good idea—so long as we're together. Where do you want to go?"

"Someplace quiet. How about Oku-Izu? We'll get up early."

"Oku-Izu? It's getting better and better."

"It'd just be a day excursion."

"What!"

"I don't want to rush things. We'll make it a day trip this time. And to prevent any misunderstandings, I want you to bring a close female friend along. You do have such a friend, don't you?"

In response to her question, Ryuji narrowed his eyes and stared as if he was looking off into the distance. "I suppose I do."

"Good. I want to be friends with her, too. You don't mind, do you?"

"OK."

"You don't seem too enthusiastic."

"What's the point if we're not alone?"

"We'll do that next time."

"Really?"

"I just can't suddenly jump into something like that. You

understand, don't you?" Yoshiko took Ryuji's hand and stroked his palm with her fingers.

"All right, it can't be helped. We'll do it your way," he conceded. "So let's set the day and time right now."

"Fine. Just wait a moment."

Yoshiko stood up and went into the office to get a train schedule.

7

Ryuji asked a woman editor at a magazine for which he did work to accompany them. He didn't explain why, but the editor, Fujiko Tasaka, agreed right away, perhaps because she could tell that he wasn't the type of guy who'd take advantage of her.

Ryuji, Yoshiko, and Fujiko arrived at Ito in Izu before noon. Their plan was to cross the mountains to Shuzenji and then return by way of Mishima.

Something was about to happen. Sensing danger, Ryuji's nerves were all taut. He was having trouble pretending nothing was wrong.

Yoshiko was calm. In one hand she carried a package—probably her lunch box—wrapped in a plastic sheet. She seemed as if she was really out to enjoy a picnic. The two women were chatting together amicably.

The bus pulled out of Ito and steadily made its way up the mountain road. As it climbed, Ito retreated into the distance, and the spring sea, tinged purple at Sagami Bay, spread out before them. Farther away, the sea dissolved into white clouds.

"My, how lovely!" The editor, oblivious of what was going on, took in the view.

Eventually, the sea, too, disappeared from sight. The bus seemed to be laboring as it crossed Amagi-renzan Pass. There were few passengers, and the majority of these, bored with the unchanging mountain scenery, had dozed off, basking in the sunlight that poured in through the windows.

"Let's get off here," said Yoshiko.

The bus stopped in the middle of the mountains. After depositing the trio, the white vehicle continued shakily down the road. Near the bus stop were four or five farmhouses, with mountains rising sharply all around.

Yoshiko's plan was to relax in the area and then take a later bus for Shuzenji.

"Let's go down this path."

Yoshiko pointed to a mountain track winding through the forest. She was in high spirits. Her forehead glistened with perspiration.

Here and there the path was wet with spring water. The trees were various shades of rich green. The silence was oppressive, almost numbing. From somewhere in the distance came the sound of a rifle shot.

The forest thinned at one spot and sunlight spilled onto the grass.

"Let's rest here," said Yoshiko. Fujiko agreed.

Ryuji looked around him. It occurred to him they had already gone quite deep into the forest. Few people would pass by here. He pictured the forests of Rinun Gorge.

"Why don't you sit down?" Yoshiko suggested to him. She had considerately spread the plastic wrapping of her lunch box over the grass. The two women sat on handkerchiefs and stretched their legs out side by side.

"I'm hungry," said the editor.

"Let's eat, then," Yoshiko responded.

The two women brought out their box lunches. Fujiko opened a cardboard box packed with sandwiches. Yoshiko took out a wooden box full of sushi. At the same time three bottles of juice tumbled out onto the grass.

Fujiko popped a sandwich into her mouth. "Try one," she offered.

"Thanks." Yoshiko helped herself to a sandwich. "I brought some sushi, but I eat it all the time and I'm kind of tired of it. Would you like some?"

She held out the small container to offer the sushi to Fujiko and Ryuji.

"Let's trade, then."

Fujiko readily accepted the box. She picked up a piece of sushi with her fingers and was about to eat it when the sushi was sent flying onto the grass.

"Stop, Fujiko."

Ryuji had knocked it out of her hand and now stood up, his face drained of blood.

"It's poisoned!"

Fujiko looked up at him, flabbergasted.

Ryuji stared at Yoshiko, whose face went pale. She glared back at him without flinching, her eyes ablaze.

"This is how you killed them at Rinun Gorge. You were the one who made it look like a lovers' suicide."

Yoshiko bit her trembling lips but remained silent. Her arched eyebrows looked contorted.

Ryuji was stuttering from excitement.

"On February eighteenth you lured Sakiji Shoda and Umeko Fukuda out to Rinun Gorge. You poisoned them by this very method, and then fled. You knew that the bodies of a man and woman would be assumed to be lovers who had committed suicide. No one would guess that a crime had taken place. And the spot, famous for the suicides of unhappy lovers, was perfect. It would all be accepted as just another suicide—nothing out of the ordinary. From the start, that's what you had in mind."

Ryuji cleared his throat and caught his breath.

8

Yoshiko didn't say a word. The editor's eyes were wide in horror. It seemed that if anyone had moved so much as an inch, the air itself would have shattered. Another rifle shot rang out in the distance.

"You carried out your plan. But one thing bothered you," Ryuji continued. "You were worried about what happened to the two. You had seen them collapse and then fled. But you wanted to know the outcome. Otherwise you'd have no peace of mind. I'm right, aren't I? Most criminals are drawn back to the scene of their crime. You did this vicariously through reading the newspaper. And you must also have wanted to know whether the police had concluded it was murder or a lovers' suicide. Tokyo newspapers wouldn't be likely to report such trifling local news. That's why you subscribed to the provincial paper. It was a clever idea.

"But you made two mistakes. When you sent in your subscription you felt you had to give some explanation. So you wrote about wanting to read my novel. You were afraid of arousing suspicion, but you went a little too far. It seemed fishy to me. Also, you asked for the paper from the nineteenth—which led me to think that the incident had occurred the day before, on the eighteenth. When I investigated, I found that you had indeed taken that day off work. I could give more details, but there's no point. After piecing the bits together, I came to the conclusion that you must have taken the express train leaving Shinjuku at 12:25. This train arrives at K. Station at 3:05. And from there you went to Rinun Gorge. As it happened, just when you arrived the minister was giving a speech to a large crowd in front of the station. The paper printed a photograph of the scene the next day. I was convinced that you would have seen this. So I decided to test you with the photograph."

Ryuji took another breath.

"I had a detective agency investigate your relationship with Sakiji Shoda. That's how I learned that the two of you had a longstanding affair. And since Sakiji had been seeing Umeko as well, everyone would assume that it was a lovers' suicide. My theory was holding up. I deliberately left the newspaper clipping with the photograph of Minister M. for you to see. And I told you a small lie. I knew it would make you suspicious of me. You see, I wanted you to know that I was putting you through a test. But I realized I needed something more effective than the clipping. The newspaper had described the clothing found on the bodies, so I had some friends of mine dress up in similar clothes, photographed them, and then showed you the photos. This must have made it perfectly clear that I was testing you. And you must have found me even more odious and menacing. Now all I had to do was wait for your invitation. And sure enough it came.

"You didn't waste any time getting closer to me so you could lure me here today, right? You asked me to bring a female friend along. That's because one body wouldn't make a lovers' suicide. If Fujiko and I ate your sushi, the cyanide or whatever you put in it would finish us off instantly. Then you would quietly leave. Three minus one. And the two corpses left in the mountains of Oku-Izu become a lovers' suicide. Everyone would have been shocked. 'You never can tell about people. Who would have thought that those two were so intimate?' they'd say. And my wife most likely would have stuffed my ashes into the closet."

Suddenly Yoshiko opened her mouth wide, and looked up, laughing hysterically.

Her laughter broke off abruptly. "Ryuji," she said sharply. "You're quite a novelist, aren't you? So you're saying this sushi is full of poison?"

"That's right," the novelist answered.

"Really? Then I'm going to eat all the sushi in the box. I want you to watch and see whether I'm poisoned or not. If it's cyanide, I'll die in three or four minutes. If it's some other poison, I'll start convulsing soon. No matter how I suffer, just leave me alone."

Yoshiko snatched the box of sushi away from Fujiko, who was in a daze. She immediately started shoving the sushi into her mouth with her fingers.

Ryuji held his breath as he watched her. He couldn't speak. All he could do was stare.

There were seven or eight pieces of sushi rolled in seaweed. One after the other Yoshiko chewed and swallowed them. It was pride, of course, that made her gobble them down with such speed.

"I've eaten them all, haven't I? Thanks to you, I'm quite full. Wait and see if I die or start convulsing." Then she stretched out on the grass.

A gentle sun shone brightly above her. She had closed her eyes. A bird was singing. Minutes passed. Ryuji and Fujiko remained by her side without saying a word. What seemed like an eternity went by.

Yoshiko seemed to be asleep, so completely still was she. But from the corners of her closed eyes two streams of tears flowed down. Ryuji was on the verge of calling to her when she jumped to her feet.

"Well, about ten minutes have gone by." She glared at Ryuji. "If it was cyanide, I'd have stopped breathing long ago. And the symptoms from other poisons would have appeared by now. But, look, I'm fit as a fiddle. I hope you realize how ridiculous your delusions were. I've never been so insulted."

She quickly wrapped the empty box and the bottles up in the plastic sheet and stood up, wiping the grass off her clothes.

"I'm leaving. Goodbye."

With these words, she strode off in the direction they had come. She seemed perfectly normal. Her firm steps soon carried her into the thick growth of the forest and out of sight.

9

This was Yoshiko's suicide note to Ryuji:

Dear Mr. Sugimoto,

My crime was exactly as you said. There is no need to correct anything. Yes, I was the one who killed them at Rinun Gorge. But why did I do it? As your detective work seems inadequate on that score, I would like to offer a final explanation.

A year before the war ended, my husband was captured in Manchuria. We had been married for less than six months. I loved him, so when I heard that with the end of the war most of the soldiers in Manchuria had been taken to Siberia, I was grief-stricken. But if he wasn't ill, I was confident that he'd return to Japan someday, and I waited patiently.

The wait seemed interminable. I don't know how many fruitless trips I took to Maizuru, where returnees disembarked, in the hope of meeting him. He had always been healthy, and believing he would return eventually, I continued to wait for him over the years. I moved from one job to another. It isn't easy for a woman to support herself, and I ended up working as a hostess at the Angel Bar in West Ginza.

The job of being a hostess requires numerous outfits. Lacking a patron, I had to struggle to buy all the clothes I needed. With my meager savings, I went to buy a dress at a department store. I bought the cheapest one I could get by with. If only I had gone home then, but no, I had a sudden urge to buy lace gloves. I went to the bargain counter, raked through the assortment, purchased a pair, and put them in my shopping bag. Then I went down to the main floor and was about to leave when a man politely asked me to step aside. It was the security guard at the department store. He asked if he could look inside my shopping bag. He took me to a place where there were no other people and then removed two pairs of gloves from my bag. One pair was wrapped, but the other wasn't. Neither did it have the seal that sales clerks put on goods sold. I was shocked. The gloves must have slipped into my bag from the counter.

I tried explaining, but he wouldn't listen. He took down my name and address in a notebook. I went pale. I was being treated like a shoplifter. Although he said I could go home, the man was smirking.

It didn't end there. Afterwards something even more upsetting happened. One day the man showed up at my apartment. He was on his way to work. He wormed his way inside and told me that this time he'd keep the matter confidential. I was overjoyed. Even though I hadn't done it deliberately, it was a relief to be spared the shame of being misjudged. The fear that word of this would get out to my neighbors or to the bar had made life a living hell for me.

When a man starts preying on a woman's weakness, you can easily imagine what course his actions will take. I was weak. I lacked courage. I was unable to resist his threats. From then on this man—Sakiji Shoda—wouldn't leave me alone. Not only did he lust after my body, he sometimes even extorted small amounts of money from me. He'd come to the bar and make me pay for his drinks. I was "keeping" him.

I blamed my husband. Why was he so long in returning? If only he had come back, I could have been spared this misery. I might have been transferring my own guilty feelings to him, since I was the one who had done wrong, but I couldn't stop myself from accusing him.

Sakiji was a despicable man, not the least like my husband. He had lots of other women. Umeko Fukuda was one of them. He even had the audacity to make us meet. He probably meant to make me jealous, hoping it would make me love him. And who can explain psychologically why I actually started to feel that way?

Before long a letter arrived from my long-silent husband. He wrote that he'd be able to return home soon. I was ecstatic. I felt as if I were looking up at a blue sky. Then I started agonizing— over Sakiji Shoda. When my husband returned, I planned to confess everything and then wait for his judgment. But first I had to cut off all ties with Sakiji. When I explained this to him, not only did he refuse to listen, but his passion seemed to grow. For this reason I resolved to murder him.

The method I used was just as you surmised. When I suggested the three of us, including Umeko, go to Rinun Gorge, Sakiji was delighted with the idea of this grotesque picnic. He felt a perverted pride in escorting two of his mistresses at once.

We arranged to take the 12:25 express from Shinjuku, but I deliberately took the earlier 11:32 local train. I didn't want the three of us to be seen together by anybody I knew. My train arrived at K. Station at 2:33. I waited thirty minutes for their express train. During that time, while eating noodles in a restaurant by the station, I saw your novel in the *Koshin News*. When I met Sakiji and Umeko, Minister M. was giving his speech in front of the station.

In the forests of Rinun Gorge I fed them home-made rice cakes laced with cyanide. They collapsed within seconds. I picked up the remaining cakes and went home, leaving behind the corpses of a lovers' suicide. Everything had gone smoothly.

I was relieved. Now I could wait for my husband's return, free from anxiety. But there was one thing bothering me. I wanted to know if the police had concluded that it was suicide or murder. That's why I subscribed to the *Koshin News*. I used your novel as an excuse, and ended up arousing your suspicions.

I wanted to be with my husband, no matter what it took, so I decided to get rid of you by the same method. But you saw through my plan. You suspected the sushi in my box lunch. Actually, I had put the poison in the juice. After you had finished the sushi, I was planning to offer you some juice to wash it down.

I took the juice back with me. It won't go to waste. It's nearly time for me to drink it.

Beyond All Suspicion

1

Dear Mr. ——

I've left out the name because I'm still debating who to send this to. I might address it to the police in charge of criminal investigations. Or maybe a suitable lawyer. Or perhaps I'll just leave it blank. I'll only be able to decide when I finish.

I'm not even sure whether this is a letter or a diary. The style is far too straightforward for a letter. But addressing it to someone is not appropriate in a diary either. Of course, by combining elements of both, perhaps I'm creating something altogether different.

First of all, I need to recount what happened seven years ago, in April 1950.

At the time I was thirty-one years old and working in Tokyo in M. Bank, one of the major Japanese banks. I was single, I lacked for nothing, and I enjoyed life. I had the usual expectations for my future.

I lived with my younger sister in a rented house on the outskirts of Asagaya. I don't know what it's like now, but in those days the neighborhood still had small patches of woodland; and if you took a deep breath you could almost smell the plains of

Musashi. Every day I would commute to work in a happy frame
of mind.

My sister, Mitsuko, was twenty-seven at the time. She had married at nineteen, but had had the bad luck to lose her husband
just as the war was about to end. I was her only sibling, so I took
her in. Luckily she didn't have any children. If a good match
could be found, I wanted her to remarry, and I was discreetly on
the lookout for her.

My sister was a cheerful person who used to sing while cleaning the kitchen and doing the wash. I'd often scold her for making such a racket. As I approached the house on my way back
from work, I could make out such songs as "Riru's Back from
Shanghai." This song was getting popular then and was a favorite
of hers. If Kasaoka from the bank were with me, I'd feel embarrassed.

"What's wrong with being cheerful?" Kasaoka looked at me
and laughed. He was about forty-two at the time; not my direct
superior but the chief of another section. Since he lived nearby,
we'd often go home together.

"Hey, act your age. You'd better watch it, singing so loudly," I
yelled at my sister from the hallway as I slid the door shut behind
me. Mitsuko stuck out her tongue.

"Am I really so old?"

"A woman close to thirty is already over the hill."

"You're awful. You don't have to add three years to my age.
Why, there are lots of people who call me 'Miss.'"

It was just as she said. Mitsuko looked young, perhaps because
of her slight build. Or perhaps because her married life had been
cut short. She had a girlish naïveté, and bright-colored clothes
suited her.

"You'll be the target of jokes if you talk like that. I was with
Kasaoka just now, and he made an odd face when he heard you
singing so loudly."

"Oh, that's impossible. Mr. Kasaoka always compliments me
on my voice. He's very friendly, isn't he? He told me that when
he first met me he thought I was twenty or twenty-one."

"Humph. You're really stuck on yourself."

My mood turned sour. My displeasure was directed not just at my sister but also at Kasaoka, who had all of a sudden become so chummy with her. Something was developing behind my back, and no matter how insignificant it might be, I didn't like the feeling of being excluded.

Even though Kasaoka was over forty, his dark brows and straight nose gave him an air of vitality. Rumor had it that his stream of women was a cause of anxiety for his wife. I needed to be careful. Thinking that I'd have to warn my sister at the first sign of anything, I was quietly keeping tabs on the situation. But nothing in particular developed. This being the case, it would have been strange to bring the subject up deliberately. On the contrary, I decided that I was worrying needlessly.

Three months later, at the end of June, Mitsuko spoke to me after breakfast.

"The day after tomorrow is the anniversary of Teruo's death. I haven't been to his grave for a long time, so I'd like to make a trip back."

Teruo, Mitsuko's late husband, was from Yamagata Prefecture. Mitsuko hadn't been there for two years.

"Of course you should go. It doesn't do not to go for so long." I gladly gave my consent. I even took out an advance on my salary that day and handed it to Mitsuko.

"It's all right. I don't need much money."

She was hesitant about taking it, but I insisted. It occurred to me afterwards that she probably really hadn't needed it.

Mitsuko was in fine spirits when she left the following morning. She must have been happy, for she had gotten up very early, while it was still dark, and had been singing her usual "Riru's Back from Shanghai" as she prepared for the trip. This time she sang softly, and I didn't scold her. When I left for work, she accompanied me as far as Shinjuku Station.

"Goodbye."

Standing on the platform, she waved to me when I was inside the packed train heading for Tokyo Station. One side of her face was bright in the morning summer sun.

That was the last time I saw Mitsuko alive.

2

Mitsuko had disappeared.

I realized this one week later, when I received the reply to the telegram I sent to her former in-laws in Yamagata. It said that Mitsuko had never arrived there. I was stunned.

Just in case, I took the express to Yamagata to confirm that she really wasn't there. The in-laws were worried, too. After some discussion, I decided to notify the police that she was missing once I got back to Tokyo. I wrote down her age, height, weight, a description of the clothes she was wearing when she left, and her distinguishing traits, and I submitted this together with a recent photograph. I was too anxious to sleep at night and kept imagining one horrible possibility after another. Half of me had pinned my hopes on the police search, while the other half had given up. I couldn't believe that the police, who must have much more important cases to deal with, would bother to investigate with any thoroughness.

I hadn't the slightest inkling why Mitsuko would leave home. She hadn't given any indication she was going to. Surely, then, she was missing not of her own free will but as a result of some factor beyond her control. I regretted letting her travel alone. True, she was twenty-seven, hardly an age where one needs an escort; and yet it seemed like a terrible oversight on my part not to have gone with her. As the days passed, I could only imagine the worst. I hurriedly subscribed to three newspapers and searched through the local news daily. I was scared, but I couldn't stop myself from looking.

It must have been around the fourth day after Mitsuko left when on my way to work I ran into Kasaoka, whom I hadn't seen for a while.

"Has your sister gone somewhere?" he asked. "Recently your door has been shut when you're not home."

"She's gone to her home town."

"Where's that?"

"In Yamagata."

At that time, I still hadn't realized that Mitsuko was missing. We stood shoulder to shoulder, hanging onto the straps in the train, making small talk as we headed for the bank.

When it came out that Mitsuko was missing, Kasaoka expressed his concern. All my colleagues in the bank knew, so there was nothing out of the ordinary in his offer of sympathy.

"How awful about your sister." He spoke in a hushed, anxious tone.

"I appreciate your concern."

"Have you asked the police to put out a search for her?"

"Yes, I've done that already."

"You can't leave it at that. I hear they'll be more thorough if you know somebody higher up," he advised me. "She's such a nice, cheerful girl. Let's hope she returns safely soon," he added by way of comforting me.

On the twenty-first day after she left home—ten days after I requested a police search—I found out what had happened to Mitsuko. The missing person's report had been effective after all.

"We've got a lead from the Y. Police Department in I. Prefecture. It wasn't an unnatural death, so we have no photograph. Will you go there?" asked the officer in charge. The town was in a famous hot spring area to the north, in the opposite direction from Yamagata. I hesitated.

"The face, body, and clothing all match. The woman died suddenly at a hot spring inn. As her identity was unknown, she was buried provisionally in the town cemetery."

I decided to go to the town and see for myself. I took the night train and arrived at noon the following day. This hot spring resort, surrounded by mountains on three sides and with a sparkling river running through the center of it, is celebrated in many folk songs; but it was to become a place of sadness for me. With a clerk from the town office to accompany me, the body was dug up from the provisional graveyard in one corner of the public cemetery. It was definitely Mitsuko. The corpse inside the coffin had decomposed, but not beyond recognition. After I made the identification, the tears came.

Stored elsewhere were her suitcase and handbag that contained her clothing, underwear, and some makeup. Everything I saw had belonged to Mitsuko.

"Is anything missing?" the clerk asked. I checked, but the only thing gone was her name card holder, which she had always carried in her handbag.

"Her name card holder isn't there."

The clerk exchanged embarrassed glances with the policemen. Someone pointed out where the identification tag had been ripped off the suitcase. It occurred to me that Mitsuko's handkerchief, embroidered with her initials, was also missing.

At last I learned what had happened. Mitsuko, who had a history of heart trouble, had suffered a sudden heart attack and died in her room at an inn. The attack occurred around five in the morning, and when the doctor rushed over an hour later her heart had already stopped beating.

"She wasn't alone," the clerk said hesitantly. I had already guessed as much, but my face turned red and I wasn't able to look at him.

I went to the inn to make my apologies for the inconvenience her death had caused. The innkeeper and the maids, with looks of embarrassment and pity, told me what had transpired.

Mitsuko and a male companion had checked in at the inn on July 1. That was the day after I parted from her at Shinjuku. She seemed to have come here straight from Tokyo. The first evening nothing had happened. Having taken a liking to the place, they stayed another night, and it was at dawn on the second night that the tragic attack occurred.

Once the commotion had begun, the man panicked. After the doctor pronounced her dead and a maid placed a white cloth over her face, the man quickly changed into his daytime clothes and dashed out of the inn. He said that he was going to the post office, and the inn people assumed that he had gone to send a telegram. In the confusion no one noticed him taking his bag or removing the name card holder from the woman's handbag. The man never returned.

They had registered under false names. A telegram sent to the address in the register was returned undelivered. The inn could do nothing but have the burial arranged by the town hall. "What an unfeeling brute." Even now the maids were speaking ill of him.

I was given a detailed description of the man and looked at his handwriting in the inn register. I paid the room charges for both of them along with a tip, and the next day I carried my sister's ashes back to Tokyo.

3

Yuichi Kasaoka was the vilest man on earth.

Mitsuko was half responsible for allowing herself to be seduced by him, so I'm not blaming him for that. But to run away after Mitsuko's sudden death at the inn was unforgivable. He was probably afraid that this unforeseen accident would expose their affair, first to his wife, then to me and the world at large. For him, Mitsuko's abrupt death had been an unexpected disaster.

I could understand the psychology behind his panicking and running away, but as Mitsuko's brother I couldn't forgive him. Even after her death, she had been abused by him. The baseness of covering his tracks by stealing her name cards and fleeing, leaving her to be buried as an unidentified corpse, made me seethe with anger. It must have been the day after he had run away that he had acted the innocent by deliberately inquiring after my sister's whereabouts. The advice he later gave me about contacting someone higher up in the police had also been just a smoke screen to hide the truth.

Both the description I was given at the inn and the handwriting in the register matched. I secretly glanced over some documents he had written at the bank; his distinctive characters were exactly the same. I found out that he had planned a week's vacation from July 1 on the pretext of visiting his home town. Everything tallied.

However, even Kasaoka did not have the gall to show up at Mitsuko's funeral. Claiming to be indisposed, he sent his wife in his place. The unknowing wife, who had a face like a fox's, prayed before the altar. I had glossed things over by saying that Mitsuko had died at a relative's. My fellow workers had seemed somewhat dubious, but I stuck to my story. I wanted to protect her reputation and my own honor. And I had another vague reason in mind.

I bumped into Kasaoka the day I was back at work after the funeral. When I asked him to come with me to the roof, his face grew pale.

There wasn't a soul on the roof. The wind was blowing, and the Tokyo streets, bathed in sunlight, spread out below us. Except for the street noises that rose up like the murmur of a distant chorus, everything seemed lifeless.

Kasaoka's face had turned as white as a sheet. I knew it wasn't just the reflection of the harsh sunlight. His features were all contorted. When I asked him about his actions in Y. Town, he refused to admit anything. He insisted that he had gone to his home town in western Japan and had not been involved in any way. I laughed.

"In that case, would you mind if I sent for the maids from the inn in Y. to meet you?" I asked. He was silent.

It took some time before he started to own up. The wind was tousling his thinning hair. "Forgive me," he said as a prelude to his confession.

He told me that his relationship with Mitsuko had become serious two months earlier and since then they had had five assignations. I was both shocked and angered at my own negligence. For a moment, I even hated Mitsuko for deceiving me. The trip had, of course, been arranged beforehand by the two. When I had given Mitsuko the advance on my salary, she was reluctant to accept it; in fact, he had paid for her share of the travel expenses.

I couldn't believe that my sister had been such a loose woman. She was a fairly extroverted person, but one part of her had been level-headed. Her married life had been brief, and after she had lost her husband and come to live with me, she rarely went out or saw friends. In short, she had remained sheltered from the world. By contrast, Kasaoka was a real womanizer; it must have been a simple task for him to seduce Mitsuko. I could easily imagine how quickly the twenty-seven-year-old Mitsuko had fallen into the clutches of this Lothario. I had feared this might happen and had kept an eye on them, so it was my fault not to have seen through them. Still, there was little good in regretting it now.

His story continued. When Mitsuko had had her first painful seizure, the startled Kasaoka was quick to wake up one of the inn employees and send him to fetch a doctor, who for some reason was slow in coming. The attacks got worse and her face turned a dark purple. While the maids ran around in confusion, all he had been able to do was panic. After a while her hands, which had been clutching her chest convulsively, stopped moving. But it wasn't until the doctor arrived that Kasaoka realized she was dead.

Kasaoka had never imagined that she would die and was reduced to a state of shock. His first reaction was fear of the repercussions. His wife mustn't find out. Mitsuko's brother must never know. The people at work had to be kept in the dark. As distraught as he was, he had managed to steal her name card holder, rip the address tag off her suitcase, and cunningly remove her monogrammed handkerchief before fleeing. At the time he had been able to think of nothing but running away. He had been like one possessed.

"Please forgive me. I was wrong. Hit me as hard as you like."

His confession over, Kasaoka's tone turned imploring.

"Hit you?"

I stared at him, flabbergasted. His conception of what constituted retribution was completely off the mark.

"Hit me all you want. In return, please don't tell anyone. If word gets out, I'll be ruined. Please, it's all I ask."

What did he mean by "ruined"? That he'd get into trouble if his wife found out? That he'd lose his job at the bank? His bloated egotism left me speechless. His notion that the incident could be settled simply by me hitting him was typical of a man who could lead a woman astray and then abandon her corpse without giving it a second thought.

If he hadn't come up with this cheap and affected "hit me," I might never have wanted to kill him.

4

I decided to murder Kasaoka. There's no need to go into my thinking in detail. In a nutshell, I detested the man. Of course, my basic motive was revenge for his having corrupted Mitsuko, but my feelings had gone way beyond that. One could say that they had soured and fermented as time passed. This Kasaoka became someone I could no longer allow to live in this world.

I considered various methods of killing him. Murder was no great problem; there are all kinds of ways to commit it. What mattered was coming up with a foolproof method so that I wouldn't be caught. Even if I accomplished my goal, what good would it do if I got caught? Revenge would be taken for my own revenge. I'd only be defeating my purposes.

I read many books on the subject. Criminals generally go to great lengths to hide their crimes. Yet despite this, in the majority of cases it is their ill-formed plans that are the cause of their undoing. Of course, almost all the cases written up in books were ones in which the criminals have been caught. But there must be many crimes still undiscovered and many murderers still at large. The perfect crime really must exist.

If I killed Kasaoka, I wouldn't try to hide his corpse. A lot of criminals have slipped up here. How foolish! All that matters is that no one knows who committed the crime.

I read a few detective novels, but they weren't of any practical use. The common denominator of such fiction was the intricacy of the tricks. They were fine for fiction, although some of them were just unbelievable, so far-fetched and labored one would have to be a magician to pull them off.

What did prove useful was the alibis. I decided a foolproof alibi was the only way to avoid being caught. Yet creating an alibi involves all sorts of chicanery. In order to account for an absence of, say, a brief twenty to thirty minutes—or, at the longest, one or two hours—one had to act like a conjurer, manipulating time, changing appearances as speedily as an actor, or employing sound-making devices such as record players. It was all very interesting but completely impractical. Such a short time span was a mistake. I had to come up with an alibi that would cover a much longer period. My decision to choose this kind of alibi was unshakable.

Then I decided that I had to remove myself as far as possible from suspicion. No matter how cleverly I acted, if I were included among the suspects, the danger factor would be that much greater. The advanced investigation and interrogation techniques of today's authorities might ultimately be my downfall. It was imperative for me to remain in a safety zone where no suspicion would cast its shadow.

When someone is murdered, the police carefully go through all his personal relationships in search of suspects. The victim's family ties, his friends, his acquaintances, both professional and private, all fall within this sphere. Once a motive is found, the suspect's actions are examined with a minuteness far surpassing his own memory. In the end, there is no escape.

I decided to place myself beyond this sphere. In other words, I would cut off all ties with Kasaoka. If I killed him now, as a colleague I would naturally come under scrutiny, and this was dangerous.

After much thought, I finally devised a plan. In order to sever ties with him, I would quit the bank. The only link between us was our place of work, so just by quitting, I'd become completely removed from his life. But it wouldn't suffice just to leave the bank. I would have to move out of Tokyo. The farther away I was from him, the less chance there was of being a suspect. It would also help to choose a new career that had nothing to do with banking.

All this would take a tremendous amount of time. As long as people remembered me, the danger factor was always present. It would be a long while before my name—Tadao Kuroi—was thoroughly erased from everyone's memory. It was absolutely necessary that I vanish in such a way that after Kasaoka's murder, no one would recall my existence. Only by fulfilling this condition would I be able to place myself completely beyond the sphere of the investigation.

I fixed this period at three years, then decided that was too risky. Even with five years I felt uneasy. In the end I decided on seven years. By that time, I would have utterly removed myself from Kasaoka's surroundings. How impetuous and restricted was the artifice of a one- or two-hour alibi. That was why it invited failure. Seven years might seem extremely long and tedious, but considering that failure would probably mean the death sentence, waiting that amount of time was nothing at all. I saw it simply as an enormous blank chunk of time. When something is too big, the conscious mind cannot grasp it.

There was one more essential condition. The motive had to remain secret—that was imperative. Luckily, there was no one who connected Kasaoka with Mitsuko's death. I hadn't told anyone, so Kasaoka and I were the only ones who knew. Kasaoka had begged me not to make it public. I would go along with his wishes. As long as it remained our secret, no one else would be able to figure out a motive.

After I had worked out my plan, I made Kasaoka a formal proposition.

"There's no point in being angry with you now. My sister loved you, so I've decided to reconcile myself to it. But for my sister's sake, I don't want you ever to tell anyone."

Kasaoka's eyes were moist with tears of gratitude.

"Really? Thank you, thank you. I deserved a thrashing from you. Thank you for your forgiveness. Of course I'll keep it a secret to the day I die."

He was the type who could say this without blushing, and so my hatred of him increased all the more. It seemed easy to be able to wait out seven years.

Kasaoka, overjoyed, became friendlier toward me. I responded as best I could. Until I quit, it wouldn't do to give the impression that we were on bad terms.

One month later, with a made-up excuse, I resigned from the bank.

5

Through a business connection, I got a job in a cement company in a town called Ube in Yamaguchi Prefecture. It was a small coastal town at the far end of Honshu. As the job had nothing to do with banking, it was ideal.

At my farewell party Kasaoka made the biggest scene. He shook my hand repeatedly and told me how much he hated to see me go. He had always been partial to alcohol, and led the others in a toast to my new career. He looked extremely happy, carrying on like this. My presence had made him uneasy after all. As I gazed at him, I guessed as much.

He saw me off at Tokyo Station, along with the rest of my colleagues. He shouted *"Banzai!"* as he waved over and over again. Who was he really cheering for? No one could have guessed the true nature of our relationship. As the lights around Shinagawa flowed past me, I bid a temporary farewell to Tokyo. Of my own volition, I was banishing myself to a distant place.

I hadn't left Tokyo, however, without taking some necessary measures. In my section at the bank there was a young man named Shigemura who had started as an office boy. I had shown special kindness to him from a long time back, so he liked me.

"Shigemura, you know I've worked here for quite a while, so even though I'm leaving the bank, I still feel close to the place. I want you to keep me posted on everyone's movements. Could you write to me if there are any changes?"

Shigemura agreed. In fact, he carried this out faithfully over the many long years. When there were any changes in personnel, he sent me the company bulletin.

I was worried that I would lose track of Kasaoka. What would be the use if I couldn't find him seven years later? Even from far away it was necessary to maintain a constant watch over him. Through Shigemura's reports I was able to keep track of Kasaoka without ever leaving home. To carry this off for seven years, I had to send Shigemura frequent gifts as tokens of my goodwill.

In this manner, I kept a low profile in the countryside for two years. Whenever I felt an urge to return to Tokyo, I suppressed it. In time I adjusted to life in the country, but my resolution remained unchanged. Occasionally someone would suggest I get married, but I never considered it. I was afraid that a change in circumstances would weaken my determination.

Three years passed, then four. Kasaoka became assistant director of the bank's Kichijoji branch, then was transferred to the branch in Meguro. Shigemura's reports kept arriving regularly. In the fifth year, Kasaoka became assistant director of the Shibuya branch.

There were two years left to go. Patiently I waited. My resolution hadn't wavered in the least. An outsider might have found me paranoid. My intense hatred of Kasaoka burned, unseen by any. The obvious motive of revenge for my sister now seemed almost minor.

There were some slight changes in my own circumstances. I was promoted to chief clerk in my company. I had also found a girl I liked, but I had made no promises of marriage. Ube was a "cement town," where white powder would come blowing over the rooftops. Beyond the houses, which looked as if they had been dusted by a fine snow, the blue sea spread out gently. On clear days you could see the mountains in Kyushu. Yet even this tranquil scenery could not weaken my resolution.

In the sixth year, Kasaoka was promoted to manager of the Omori branch. One more year left. Six years was a long time after all.

I had removed myself completely from Kasaoka's surroundings. No matter how his circle was widened, there was no way the name Tadao Kuroi would surface. I had cut off all ties with him, both temporal and spatial. Whatever mishap might befall Kasaoka, there was no longer anyone who would recall my existence. I had vanished from the scene without leaving a trace.

Toward the end of the sixth year, Kasaoka was transferred to the Nakano branch. And to make things more convenient, Shigemura had become a teller there. Shigemura's letter contained the following information: "Mr. Kasaoka, now branch manager, has become an even heavier drinker. Almost every night he makes the rounds of the bars behind Shinjuku's Niko Building."

For me, this was an invaluable tip on the movements of the enemy.

At last the seventh year came. Time had passed slowly, and the seven years weighed heavily on me. Time had taken on an almost physical presence. In my own way, I was happy that my resolution had remained steadfast over the years.

Around April, I put in a request at work for a two-week vacation. Two weeks might not be necessary, but I was calculating the time it could take to find Kasaoka. Once we met, the deed would be accomplished within an hour. As soon as it was over I intended to leave Tokyo. This was the plan I had perfected seven years earlier, when I had quit my job at the Tokyo bank.

I had already gotten hold of the cyanide. It had been easy to obtain it through a connection at the factory. It was the best method, I decided, quick and effective.

I tucked this away in my pocket, and eagerly headed for Tokyo.

When I got off at Tokyo Station, I was surprised by the changes that had taken place in seven years. There were any number of tall buildings that hadn't been there before. It was a great city after all. My long absence had made me nostalgic, and yet I realized that, at the same time, I was no longer in touch with anything. I had been worn down by seven years of country life. My face reflected in the shop windows had aged. I had wasted the latter half of my youth. Still, I had no regrets, for at the end of my exile lay my long-desired goal—Kasaoka.

I thoroughly familiarized myself with the timetables for trains leaving Tokyo Station. As soon as I arrived, I had to make my plans for escape.

In the evening I took a room in a small inn in Kanda, close to both Shinjuku and Tokyo Station. It was an inconspicuous place.

6

That evening I roamed the Kabuki-cho night life area behind Shinjuku's Niko Building. I walked from ten until nearly midnight. This was the time when I was most likely to encounter the carousing Kasaoka. In fact, there were many people of his type walking about. It really didn't matter who might see me, for I was a mere traveler in the crowd, and there was no one who would know me. Who could say where I had wandered in from? Tadao Kuroi—a securities clerk at the Tokyo main office of M. Bank seven years ago—no longer existed.

That evening I did not find Kasaoka. It would have been too much of a windfall to have run into him on the first night after my arrival. The next day, I hardly set foot out of the inn during the daytime. One can't be too cautious. I was guarding against the faintest possibility of running into someone I knew.

However, one could say that this was an unnecessary precaution. Even if I did run into an old, neglected acquaintance, surely there'd be no one who'd link me to Kasaoka's murder. The threads connecting us had been completely severed. There was the distance of seven years and 1,050 kilometers. I no longer appeared anywhere in Kasaoka's surroundings. I was simply being overly cautious by not going out in the daytime.

Again the next evening I prowled around Shinjuku, but in vain. This time I felt a bit apprehensive. Could he possibly be sick or away on a business trip? In that case, I'd be better off going home after a week. I could set out again another time. I wasn't the least bit disappointed. Compared to the strain of waiting seven years, this delay was nothing at all.

The following evening I realized that I had been worrying needlessly. At 10:27 I clearly made out Kasaoka's figure leaving a bar in the street behind the Niko Building.

When I spotted him I didn't get especially excited. Perhaps the impact was so great that, conversely, I was struck by a wave of calmness. He was walking a bit unsteadily; I tapped him on the shoulder, acting as if no time had passed. His baldness had spread as far as the back of his head.

"Mr. Kasaoka, it's been ages," I said calmly. Then, for the first time, emotion came welling up inside me. Kasaoka didn't seem able to recall me easily. He was probably struggling to figure out which of his clients this smiling face in front of him belonged to.

But that didn't last long. A look of surprise appeared on his face; then, in the characteristic manner of drunks, he flung out both arms wildly, and shook me heartily by the shoulders.

"Hey, it's Kuroi, right?"

His bulging eyes were proof that his shock hadn't worn off yet. "Hey!" he repeated. He seemed uncertain what to say next.

"It's been a long time. I'm glad to see you're well."

I had to suppress my surging emotions and, holding my smile, I tried to calm him down. We were in the middle of the street. People weaved around us in droves. None of the pedestrians paid us any special attention.

"When did you come here?" Kasaoka finally asked. He must also have been overcome by complex emotions, but he was keeping them hidden.

"I just got here. I haven't been back for a while. Tokyo is getting more and more prosperous," I answered. At last he regained his normal drunken expression.

"Tokyo's gone downhill—too many people and too many cars," he said. In seven years his physical appearance had gotten more imposing, and his manner of speaking had taken on an air of importance befitting a bank branch manager.

"Oh, by the way, I hear you've been made branch manager— my belated congratulations." I had said it without thinking, meaning to flatter him. Kasaoka looked at me.

"Who told you that?" he asked in response. I was taken aback.

"Oh, I just heard it somewhere. How nice for you," I added quickly. Since he was being complimented, Kasaoka didn't harp on the matter. His mood improved greatly.

"Let's have a drink somewhere and catch up on things," he said.

I breathed a sigh of relief. From now on I'd have to watch what I came out with. I chastised myself for being careless.

I had been waiting for Kasaoka to invite me out for a drink. This was the very chance I had been hoping for. Everything was going as planned.

"How many years has it been?" Kasaoka asked cheerfully as we walked. He seemed to have lost all sense of time.

"Seven years."

"Seven years? That long, eh?" Those inadvertent words made my hatred for him flare up. He obviously couldn't understand the substance and weight of seven years. I had quit the bank and exiled myself to the distant countryside because of this man. Half of my life had been ruined. As I glanced at his broad shoulders, I knew the time had come to have him taste my revenge.

"Oh, Mr. Kasaoka," I said casually. "When we get to the bar, let's not bring up meeting after seven years. I'm still not quite over my memories from then."

That seemed to get through to him.

"Fine with me. Let's just drink together like normal."

7

The first bar we entered was large and full of customers. The conditions were good. The more crowded the better.

Kasaoka seemed to be a regular there, and waitresses who passed by cast him smiling glances.

"Is your job interesting?" he asked.

"Not especially, but the pace is easy in the country."

"That's what matters. Wearing out your nerves every day like I do is for the birds."

He said this a bit boastfully. As he poured the beer, he kept urging me to drink. He was drunk, and I pretended to be drunk, too.

It was strange indeed to have the man I had kept track of from the western tip of Honshu all these years sitting right in front of me. It was so bizarre it might have been an illusion. At moments I couldn't help thinking that he was unreal.

Suddenly he started to sing. He was singing so softly and slowly that I couldn't make it out at first, but when he raised his voice, I found myself staring at him. The song was "Riru's Back from Shanghai."

So he, too, must have had to listen to Mitsuko singing the song ad infinitum. Or perhaps she had taught it to him. And it was likely that seeing her brother had brought it all back. His face bright red, he continued singing it sluggishly, taking big gasps of breath. I felt a little sad, perhaps because I was a bit drunk. At some point, I also started to sing, in time to his beat.

" 'Riru, Riru, where are you, Riru?/Does anyone know where Riru is?' As I sang, I could almost hear Mitsuko's voice and my own scolding of her to be quiet. Tears flowed down my cheeks.

"It's a nice song, isn't it?" Kasaoka seemed lost in the past. "The song had just gotten popular at the time. It all comes back, doesn't it?"

A young waitress walking by at that moment glanced at Kasaoka and then turned her gaze on me. It was only for an instant, but I was sure that she heard what Kasaoka said. The proof was that she also began singing "Riru, Riru" as she walked. I felt sick. It was a dark moment, like passing through a tunnel.

I had to make a move quickly. Kasaoka was leaning on the table, his eyes closed, on the verge of falling asleep. His glass was still half full of beer. The place was bustling with people, none of whom were looking our way.

From my pocket I took out a paper sachet of the type used to hold medicine and opened it. The small pile of white powder resembled crushed aspirin. I folded the paper in half with my fingertips, took Kasaoka's glass, and tipped the paper up while hiding the glass under the table. The white powder slipped down pleasingly and dissolved in the yellow brew. My heartbeat remained steady as I returned the glass to the table and quickly filled it with beer. The cloudy mixture disappeared inside the foam.

"Mr. Kasaoka," I called out. I tapped his shoulder. He lifted his head and half-opened his bloodshot eyes.

"Let's make a toast."

I poured beer into my own glass and raised it high. He made a kind of grunt as he reached for the glass in front of him. After lifting it to his lips, his mouth puckered a bit. I held my breath, but there was nothing to worry about. He gulped it all down. His obligation evidently fulfilled, he once more let his head droop onto the table. In about one minute he would start writhing. I put on my shoes and went outside, as if to get some air. Once out I made off, taking big strides. In four or five minutes he would breathe his last. The crucial act had been carried out as if it were nothing at all. It was too ridiculous. People were laughing and talking as they walked, just like before—indifferent and unconcerned. Once more I had become an anonymous visitor to Tokyo.

According to my watch, it was three minutes past eleven. I remembered that there was a train leaving for Osaka at 11:35. I had just enough time to return to the inn and get ready. I hailed a cruising taxi, and as I got inside I called out "Kanda" briskly.

The cab picked up speed as it pulled away from "the scene of the crime." By now Kasaoka would have left this world. The seven years of emotion felt too light; a sense of fulfillment was missing. As I took in the breeze from the window, it vaguely occurred to me that it would probably be a while before the reality sank in.

Dear Mr. ——

I sense that the time is approaching for me to fill in the blank with a name. I still can't quite come to a decision. I have to write a bit more.

On the night train back I considered whether I had made any slip-ups. I went over everything minutely, but I couldn't find any mistakes. Although I was more or less satisfied, I felt that a tiny crack had been left somewhere. This crack in its small way stubbornly marred my complacency and made me feel uneasy.

The sea on my left was devoid of lights. As I gazed at the pitch black scenery, I suddenly figured out where the crack was: the eyes of the waitress when we were drinking. The dark foreboding I had felt then was still dogging me. I shook my head. Don't worry. You're getting all worked up over nothing. There's no reason to feel uneasy. Calm down, calm down, I kept telling myself.

I was in a zone of absolute safety. I was completely removed from Kasaoka's surroundings. No matter how the authorities looked into his personal relations, there was no way I'd appear in their investigation. How could they dig up someone who had left his place of work seven years ago? The employees who'd be asked to give statements wouldn't even recall the first letter of my name. Since no robbery was involved, the authorities would investigate all his illicit relationships and personal enemies. But no one knew of this. I had been wiped off everyone's memory. My face had been seen at the bar, but that was nothing to worry about. It was crowded, and who'd pay attention to a new customer? Even if the witness could recall my features, I was just a visitor to Tokyo. There was no way the authorities could locate me from her description. I was someone who no longer existed in anyone's memory. It had taken many years and meticulous planning to obtain this sense of immunity. The sacrifice had involved much pain and perseverance.

A letter came from Shigemura informing me that Kasaoka had been poisoned by cyanide, but the motive for the murder remained unknown. I felt relieved.

However, today, three weeks later, I found out that a detective had been making inquiries about me at the general affairs section. He had been asking persistent questions about my one-week vacation. When I heard this from a friend in the section, I instantly came up against the eyes of the bar waitress. The premonition I had had was about to become reality. I suddenly understood it all.

It was when Kasaoka and I had been singing "Riru's Back from Shanghai." Afterwards, he had said emotionally, "The song had just gotten popular at the time. It all comes back, doesn't it?" The waitress had heard this. Then she had turned to look at me. I had also been singing "Riru." She would have told the police that. Kasaoka had been a regular there, and waitresses tend to notice customers their regulars bring with them.

The investigators must have concluded that the murderer and victim had known each other when "Riru" had gotten popular— in other words, in 1950. The net would be tightened. When they got that far, the rest would fall into place. It would be easy to match up the waitress's description of Kasaoka's companion with one of the employees at M. Bank in 1950.

Both my careful plans and the seven years of perseverance collapsed in an instant. I laughed aloud. Mitsuko's "Riru" had been my downfall. What an annoying song it was, after all!

I'm too tired to write any more. But I want to say that even though I was defeated I have no regrets. Any moment now the detective will probably come knocking on my door. Undoubtedly, he'll have a warrant for my arrest in his pocket.

Should I address this to the head of investigations or to a lawyer? Or should I turn this into a will made out to no one? With only a few minutes left, I still can't decide.

The Voice

PART 1
The Wrong Number

1

Tomoko Takahashi worked as a telephone operator in a newspaper company. Since she alternated day and night shifts with the seven or eight other switchboard operators, she was required to work overnight every three days.

It was Tomoko's shift that night. The operators worked in groups of three, but after eleven o'clock two would nap while one stayed on duty. This would rotate on an hourly basis.

Tomoko was sitting by the switchboard reading a book. When one o'clock came, she would go wake up one of the operators sleeping on a mattress in a small adjoining room. Before then, I can read about fifteen pages, she thought to herself. Since it was an interesting novel, she made a mental note of this while she read.

Just then there was an outside call. Tomoko looked up from her book.

"The city desk, please." Since she recognized the speaker's voice, she did not hesitate to connect the call.

"There's a call from Mr. Nakamura," she relayed to Ishikawa at the city desk, who had answered the phone in a sleepy voice.

Then she returned to her world of fiction. After a while the call ended.

She hadn't read more than two pages when the red light in front of her blinked. It was an inside call.

"Hello."

"Ring up Professor Makio Akaboshi from the University of Tokyo."

She recognized the caller's voice: it was Hiroshi Ishikawa, assistant chief of the city desk. In contrast to his sleepy voice a few minutes earlier, he now sounded quite lively.

Tomoko could distinguish almost all the voices of the company's three hundred employees. An operator generally has a good ear, but in the opinion of her colleagues Tomoko's ability was exceptional. She'd only have to hear a voice two or three times to remember it.

"It's Mr. So-and-so, isn't it?" She'd be able to guess who it was even before the caller had a chance to give his name. Those who had called only a few times before were taken by surprise.

"You've got quite a memory," they'd exclaim.

Sometimes, however, it caused problems for the men at the newspaper; the operators could also remember the voices of their women callers.

"Mr. A.'s girlfriend's name is H. She's got a husky, stuck-up voice."

"Mr. B.'s girl is Y., right?"

They'd even remember the bar hostesses—hardly what you'd call girlfriends—who'd call to pester the men to pay their bills. Of course, the operators would never do anything as unethical as to divulge these so-called professional secrets to others. But they enjoyed whispering about them in the switchboard room to help pass the time. These operators could distinguish the slightest peculiarity, intonation, and pitch of hundreds of voices.

Tomoko started thumbing through the thick telephone directory. Her fingertips slid expertly down the listing of names starting with "a" until she found Makio Akaboshi. "Forty-two, six-seven-two-one," she said to herself.

She dialed. The ringing tone from the receiver tickled her ear.

The clock on the wall said 12:23. The phone continued ringing, and Tomoko pictured it echoing in the sleeping house.

Just as she was beginning to think it would be a while before somebody woke up and answered, the receiver was picked up after a surprisingly short time.

Later, when Tomoko was questioned by the police, she replied that it took about fifteen seconds for the party to come on the line.

"How do you know the exact time?" she was also asked.

"I was concerned about calling so late at night."

Although the receiver had been picked up, no one spoke immediately. A few eerie seconds of silence passed as if the person was debating whether to answer or not. She had to say "Hello" three or four times before there was a reply.

"Who is it?" asked a man's voice.

"Is this Professor Akaboshi's residence?"

"You've got the wrong number." He seemed about to hang up, so Tomoko quickly asked, "I'm sorry, but isn't this the residence of Professor Makio Akaboshi from the University of Tokyo?"

"I told you, wrong number."

He didn't speak loudly, but his voice was gruff. Tomoko wondered whether she had looked up the wrong number or had made a mistake dialing. She was about to apologize when he added, "This is the crematorium."

Despite the deepness of the voice, the tone had an oddly tinny ring to it.

Tomoko knew right away that what he had said was untrue. When she dialed a wrong number, she was often told it was the jail, the crematorium, the tax office, or some such disagreeable place. She should have been used to these jokes, but this time she felt annoyed.

"How rude of you. You're not the crematorium. Don't be stupid," she shot back.

"Sorry. But you shouldn't be dialing wrong numbers in the middle of the night. What's more . . ."

Before he could continue, the line suddenly went dead. Her intuition told her that another person had cut them off.

The brief exchange had lasted less than a minute. But her mood had suddenly darkened as if someone had smeared it with black ink. Since she couldn't see their faces when she talked to people on the phone, her job was hard on the nerves at times.

Once more Tomoko leafed through the directory. Sure enough, she had made a mistake. She had dialed the number below the one she wanted. This almost never happened.

What's wrong with me tonight? Was I too wrapped up in my book, she wondered as she dialed the correct number.

The phone kept ringing. This time, however, no one answered.

A call came from Ishikawa, urging her to hurry up. "Hey, haven't you gotten him yet?"

"He must be asleep already. He won't get up, it seems."

"Dammit. Just keep ringing."

"What? So late at night?"

Tomoko was on familiar terms with Ishikawa so she was able to voice her doubts freely.

"A famous scholar just died. I want to get a comment from Akaboshi over the phone."

The deadline for the morning edition was one o'clock. Now she could understand Ishikawa's impatience.

The phone rang for five minutes before it was finally picked up. Tomoko connected Akaboshi to Ishikawa.

The green light on the switchboard, which indicated that the line was busy, kept glowing tirelessly. Ishikawa was probably listening intently. The color of the light reminded her of the jade ring Shigeo Kotani had given her recently.

2

They had bought it together at a store in Ginza. Shigeo was about to walk boldly into the place, but Tomoko hesitated.

"It's bound to be expensive if we buy a ring in such a fancy shop."

"Don't worry. In the long run quality pays off. We can't help it being a bit expensive." Brushing her misgivings aside, he had entered the store. Tomoko was overawed by the ostentatiousness of the shop. She had him buy the cheapest ring she could find among the expensive price tags. Even so, it cost considerably more than what she would have paid at an ordinary store.

Shigeo was like that. In spite of the fact that he worked at an unknown, third-rate company and was always complaining of his pittance of a salary, he'd have fashionable clothes made for himself on credit, buy new ties all the time, and spend as much as 800 yen to take Tomoko to a movie in a posh Yurakucho theater. He always seemed to be in debt. Both his foppishness and the unstable side to his nature was a source of concern for Tomoko.

Even to a fiancé, it can be surprisingly difficult to speak one's mind. Tomoko blamed this on her own timidity. Until they got married there was nothing she could do about it. Women had this weakness in their character. The fact that she was in love with him might also have something to do with it. She vaguely hoped that she'd be able to correct his spendthrift habits once they settled into married life.

Shigeo's pale complexion and lustreless eyes seemed to lack vitality. Listening to his constant complaints and hearing nothing of his dreams or ambitions made Tomoko feel uneasy about him.

The green light in front of her blinked off cheerlessly, signaling that Ishikawa's long phone call had come to an end. Tomoko glanced up absently at the wall clock. There were seven minutes left of her shift. In five minutes she could wake up the other operator.

The telephone book still lay open. She had the sudden urge to look at the name belonging to 42-6721, the wrong number she had dialed. The rudeness still rankled, as though she had been spat on.

Shinzo Akaboshi, 7-263 Setagaya-cho, Setagaya Ward.

Shinzo Akaboshi. What did he do, she wondered. When she was in high school Tomoko had occasionally visited a friend who lived around there, so she knew the area. It was an upper-class residential district, crisscrossed with white walls beyond which huge roofs could be glimpsed hidden inside wooded gardens.

It was hard to reconcile the owner of that uncouth voice with such a fancy neighborhood. True, after the war incongruities of this kind had become commonplace. The uneducated, vulgar quality of the man's voice had brought this fact home to her with renewed force. It was the lack of harmony of the deep voice and its tinny tone that left her with such an unpleasant impression.

At ten in the morning, when her shift was over, Tomoko went home. She was in the habit of staying up until the afternoon, and went to bed at one o'clock, after cleaning the house and doing the laundry.

When she awoke, the light dangling from the ceiling was already lit. It was completely dark outside the sliding glass windows. The evening paper lay by her side. Her mother always left it there for her.

Tomoko reached for the paper to wake herself up.

"WIFE OF COMPANY DIRECTOR MURDERED IN SETAGAYA
LATE AT NIGHT WHEN HUSBAND AWAY"

The headline across the front page immediately did away with her sleepiness. The article went as follows: "When company director Shinzo Akaboshi of 7-263 Setagaya-cho, Setagaya Ward, returned home by taxi at approximately 1:10 this morning, he found that his wife, Masae (29), had been strangled. Akaboshi had been away attending a relative's funeral since the previous night, leaving his wife alone in the house. As the house had been ransacked, it was evidently a case of robbery. The police suspect that more than one person was involved, although this is not certain. A nephew of the couple, a student living nearby, had visited the house with a friend, but due to the lateness of the hour, they left at 12:05. The murder is thought to have occurred between then and the discovery of the body at 1:10."

Tomoko screamed.

3

When Tomoko appeared at the Setagaya police station that was handling the investigation, the detective in charge asked her why she thought the voice on the phone had been that of the murderer.

"According to the newspaper article, the deceased was alone between 12:05 and 1:10. It was 12:23 when I dialed the house by mistake. A man's voice came on the line. Considering the time, it seems to me that it might have been the criminal."

"What did he say?"

Tomoko recounted the details.

The officer seemed extremely interested in the fact that the call had been cut short, giving the impression that somebody next to the speaker had broken the connection.

He had her go over this point in detail, and then spoke in a low voice to the other policemen present. Later she realized that this provided a vital clue as to whether the murder was committed by one person or more.

"What kind of voice was it?" the detective asked. He divided voices into categories of shrill, low, middle-range, harsh, thick, and clear, and asked her which elements were strongest.

Tomoko was at a loss for an answer. She couldn't sum up the voice in words. It would be oversimplifying to call it a deep voice. Even with deep voices, there were probably one or two thousand different levels. To say "a deep voice" would be to give the detective only the most general idea. That wouldn't do. If she said he had "a deep, hoarse" voice, she could convey a certain impression, but when the voice had no characteristic as distinct as "hoarse," how could she describe it? It was impossible to convey sensations accurately through words.

Understanding Tomoko's quandary, the detective gathered together a few people and had them recite something short. Since she said "a deep voice," he chose only those that fit that description. Tomoko was reminded once again that a lot of men have deep voices.

The men looked embarrassed as they read out loud. After listening to all of them, she said that there were some she thought were close, but on further reflection they were very different. It was the only reply she could make. Alike and different at the same time.

"In that case . . ." The detective tried a new approach. "You're a telephone operator, so you're used to listening to voices, right?"

"Yes."

"How many voices can you distinguish among your company's employees?"

"Hmm, about three hundred perhaps."

"That many?"

The startled detective exchanged glances with the police officer next to him.

"Then, from among those three hundred, whose voice resembles his the most?"

It was a clever idea. Out of three hundred workers, there had to be a voice that more or less matched. This way they'd be able to get something more specific. Tomoko was impressed.

However, the flip side was that being specific made it impossible for her to match up voices. All she could say conclusively was that A.'s voice and B.'s voice had their respective characteristics.

Oddly enough, the voice on the phone was beginning to recede from her memory. She had been made to recall too many voices, and the voice in question was getting buried under the pile.

In the end, the only rather inconsequential piece of evidence the authorities were able to gather from Tomoko was that the criminal had "a deep voice."

But the story was played up by all the newspapers. Headlines such as "MURDERER'S VOICE AT THE SCENE OF THE CRIME; TELEPHONE OPERATOR'S ACCIDENTAL MIDNIGHT CALL" appeared along with Tomoko's name. For a while she was either an object of curiosity or the butt of jokes.

One month passed, then two. The articles in the newspapers kept getting shorter until they were relegated to the bottom corner of the page.

Nearly six months later, after a long silence, a slightly larger article appeared saying that the investigating team had been disbanded with the murderer's identity still unknown.

4

One year later, Tomoko left her job to begin married life with Shigeo Kotani.

After their marriage, the doubts that Tomoko had previously felt about Shigeo turned into reality.

Shigeo was an idler who'd go to work when the mood struck him. He'd complain incessantly about his company.

"I'd quit that job tomorrow," he'd say when drinking. He'd then brag about how he could get a better salary somewhere else. But Shigeo's abilities did not match his idle boasts, as Tomoko realized once they were married.

"It'll be the same wherever you work. Just because you're not completely satisfied, there's no reason to slack off. At least go to work every day."

Tomoko's attempts at encouragement were met with scornful laughter. "You've got no idea how a man feels about his job," he'd reply.

Three months later, he actually did quit his job.

"What are you going to do now?" Tomoko was crying.

"Oh, something'll turn up," he said puffing on a cigarette. He liked acting the tough guy, even though he was a weakling at heart.

For the next six months they lived on the brink of poverty. The better jobs that Shigeo had talked about were nowhere to be found. He started to panic. With no practical skills, he was a pitiful case. Both his physical condition and his vanity prevented him from working as a laborer. Finally he got a job as an insurance salesman through a newspaper ad or something, but considering his personality it was a foregone conclusion that he wouldn't last very long. He quit before he even got his first commission.

However, to put it in Shigeo's words, his "luck changed" and he landed a new job. He said he got it through some acquaintances he made on his insurance route. They planned to form a small trading company dealing in medical supplies, and since Shigeo had no capital, he'd "invest" his own labor.

Tomoko didn't quite understand what this meant, but in any case Shigeo happily set off for work every day. He told her the company was located near Nihonbashi, but she never went there.

At the end of the month, however, Shigeo duly handed over

his salary. It was quite a large sum. Oddly, the name of the company wasn't printed on the envelope, nor was there any receipt. Tomoko, who was familiar with monthly wage packets, thought it strange, but concluded that the company's practices were just different. In any event, she was delighted to have some money at last.

Although love is said to be the basis of married life, to Tomoko it seemed that economic stability was the real root. She could not count the number of times she had resolved to leave Shigeo during their six months of poverty. She had exhausted all her love for her indolent husband, and every time they quarreled, she invariably thought of running away.

When his salary started coming in regularly again, peace was restored between them. It was strange to Tomoko how love could be swayed by money in a marriage, but in reality she had completely gotten over her melancholy.

The company seemed to be doing well. Shigeo got a slight increase in pay in his third month and another raise the following month. They were able to pay back their debts and even had enough left over to buy some new clothes and furnishings.

"Tomoko, is it all right if I invite some of the guys from work over for mahjongg?" Shigeo asked. Tomoko was delighted.

"I'd love it. But our place is so small, it's embarrassing."

"What difference does that make?"

"I'll fix lots to eat then," she said cheerfully. As they were important guests from her husband's office, she wanted to do whatever she could.

The following evening three men came. One was over forty, and the other two looked to be in their early thirties. Contrary to her expectations, they weren't very refined. She had been told they were in management, and she had formed her own impression of what they'd be like; but in reality they looked more like salesmen.

The forty-odd-year-old man was called Kawai. The other two introduced themselves as Muraoka and Hamazaki.

"Sorry to intrude like this," Kawai greeted her. He was balding, with narrow eyes, thin lips, and prominent cheekbones. Muraoka's long hair, stiff with pomade, was combed back. Hamazaki had a red face, as if flushed from drinking.

Muraoka, the youngest of them, was carrying the case of mahjongg tiles and the table. They stayed up all night playing mahjongg.

Tomoko didn't get any sleep that night. Around midnight she fixed them a curry.

"You shouldn't have bothered," said the older Kawai, bowing to her. There was something friendly about his tiny eyes.

After the meal, she served them tea. Once that was taken care of, Tomoko went to bed. It was close to one o'clock.

However, she couldn't get to sleep. Their home was so small that Tomoko had no choice but to spread out her bedding in the room next to where they were playing. She could hear everything through the sliding doors. They were trying to keep their voices down so they wouldn't disturb her, but when they got excited they'd yell out, "Oh, hell!" or "Dammit!" and there were occasional bursts of laughter, or voices loudly figuring out scores. She could put up with that to a certain extent, but what really drove her up the wall was the clattering of the tiles as they were shuffled. It grated on her nerves.

Tomoko kept tossing and turning. She tried plugging her ears up, but the more she tried not to let the sound bother her, the worse it got.

She wasn't able to sleep a wink until dawn.

5

Mahjongg must exert some uncanny fascination. After that evening, Shigeo would often invite Kawai, Muraoka, and Hamazaki over to the house.

"Sorry to barge in like this."

"Appreciate your hospitality."

Tomoko was forced to act the gracious hostess. Since her husband was obligated to these men from his company, she couldn't show any displeasure.

"Please come in. Really, it's no inconvenience."

All the same, at night she would have to prepare a snack. That in itself was all right. The bad part was what followed. The voices calling out *"che!"* and *"pon!"*, the muffled laughter, and the sound of the tiles being knocked down and shuffled were more than she could take. Just when she'd finally dozed off, the clattering of tiles would wake her up again. Her nerves were shot to pieces.

After this had continued for a while, she ended up complaining about it to Shigeo.

"I don't mind you playing mahjongg, but I can't stand them coming here all the time. I can't sleep a wink. I'm on the verge of a breakdown."

Shigeo made a sour face.

"You can put up with that much. I owe Kawai all I've got. You yourself seem pretty pleased with my salary."

"Of course, but . . ."

"Look, it's all part of society's game. Even if I hate mahjongg, it's my duty to hang out with them." Then he added reassuringly, "Just try to bear with it. I was the one who first invited these guys over. They're delighted to come, and they're always going on about how good-natured you are. It's not every night, so try to be patient. We'll move somewhere else before long."

Tomoko was forced to agree. But she felt a little as if she was being coaxed into something while being kept in the dark.

Come to think of it, she knew next to nothing about Kawai and the others. When she asked Shigeo about them, he would just laugh and make some vague reply. She also had no idea as to exactly what kind of business they were in. But one part of Tomoko was afraid to press Shigeo too closely. The misery she had gone through when they had no money had left its mark. The stability brought on by his decent salary made her fear the consequences of its loss. She had a vague foreboding that if she pressed the matter too far, her life might fall apart.

In the last analysis, she made a pretense of accepting Shigeo's scanty explanations, although she couldn't place much trust in them. She knew she was deceiving herself, and this left her with an awful feeling, like waking up bathed in cold sweat.

Even on nights when there was no mahjongg, Tomoko was finding it hard to sleep. She started taking small doses of tranquilizers.

It happened three months later.

On that day, too, the men were to play mahjongg. Kawai and young Muraoka had already come, but Hamazaki was late. For a while they made small talk with Shigeo, but for some reason the red-faced Hamazaki still didn't show up.

"Where the hell is he? What a jerk!" Muraoka, his long pomaded hair glistening, was already angry.

"Don't get impatient or you'll wind up losing. He'll be here before long." Kawai, with his tiny eyes and thin lips, was trying to be encouraging; but, in fact, he was also getting irritated.

"What on earth could have happened?" Shigeo looked put out.

"How about playing three-handed mahjongg until Hamazaki gets here?" Kawai suggested.

"Great idea." Muraoka, who was bored to death, was open to anything.

The three started playing. They seemed to be enjoying themselves amid shouts of *"che!"* or *"pon!"*

"Excuse me." A woman who ran the neighborhood grocery store was at the front door.

"You have a telephone call," she told Tomoko. "It's from a Mr. Hamazaki." Tomoko thanked her and relayed the message.

"Damn Hamazaki. What a nerve he has, calling like this," Kawai muttered as he picked up his tiles.

Shigeo called out to Tomoko. "I can't get away now, so you go."

Tomoko ran to the store where there was a phone in the back. The owner seemed annoyed, and Tomoko apologized as she put the receiver to her ear.

"Hello." She spoke in the polished tone that she had acquired at her former job.

"Hello. Oh, Mrs. Kotani? It's me, Hamazaki."

"Oh . . ."

Tomoko's hand on the receiver suddenly tensed.

"Please pass on a message to Mr. Kawai. Tell him some unavoidable business came up today so I won't be able to come over. Hello . . ."

"Yes . . ."

"Did you hear me?"

"Yes, yes . . . I'll give him the message."

She put the receiver back in a daze. She didn't even notice leaving the store. The voice just now, Hamazaki's voice, it was that voice from three years ago; that voice on the phone when late one night she had accidentally called a house where a murder had just taken place! That unforgettable brutish voice.

6

Her head still spinning, Tomoko managed to give Hamazaki's message to Kawai. She cowered by the back door as if she was hiding from somebody. Her heart was pounding.

The voice was still ringing in her ears. It wouldn't leave her, like some kind of aural hallucination. There was no doubt it was the same voice. She could trust her own ears, she was confident of that. Hadn't everyone always praised her ear for voices? Her sense of hearing had been professionally trained. If it was a voice on the telephone, she could easily distinguish an infinite number of variations.

Until then, she had often heard Hamazaki's voice. She'd hear it every time he came to play mahjongg. Why hadn't she noticed it before? How had his voice managed to get by her? Was it because she had been hearing his voice in person rather than through the telephone receiver?

That must be the reason, she realized.

A voice heard live is very different from one heard over the telephone. If it's somebody you know well, you'll come to hear them as the same, but it's not that way at first. Even the tone will seem different. The reason Tomoko hadn't remembered Hamazaki's voice when he came to play mahjongg was because she was hearing it firsthand. It was only when she heard him over the telephone that she recognized it as the voice of that midnight phone call.

The three stopped playing mahjongg.

"This isn't any fun. Half the excitement is gone with only three."

Kawai lit a cigarette and stood up.

"Damn Hamazaki," cursed Muraoka as he returned the tiles to the case. Shigeo couldn't see Tomoko anywhere and shouted for her.

Kawai suddenly cut him short. "Your wife's name is Tomoko?" he asked. Shigeo, who rarely called his wife by name, looked embarrassed.

"How do you write it?"

"With the character for 'morning.'"

At once Kawai's eyes clouded over. He seemed about to ask something else when Tomoko appeared, causing him to stop short.

"Oh, are you leaving already?"

Kawai looked casually at Tomoko from the corners of his small eyes. He might have noticed that her complexion was paler than usual.

"With one person missing, we can't get in the mood. Thanks for your hospitality."

As the senior member, Kawai was his usual courteous self. He left with Muraoka. Tomoko saw them off at the cramped hallway as she always did. But on this occasion her expression was stiff. The men walked away without looking back.

"What's wrong?" Shigeo stared at Tomoko.

"Nothing." She couldn't tell her husband. He was keeping something from her, and although she had no idea what it was, she sensed it with a wife's intuition. In short, her husband was on their side, and she feared that opening up to him would make her vulnerable. Wherever she looked, she saw Hamazaki's flushed face.

Oddly enough, that was the last time they came to play mahjongg.

"What happened?" she asked Shigeo.

"You were making a face, weren't you?" he replied angrily.

"What do you mean?" Her heart skipped a beat.

"Mr. Kawai said that we were imposing on you too much, so we should play somewhere else.

"I didn't make any faces."

"You've always resented our mahjongg games. It showed on your face. That's why Mr. Kawai got put off."

Shigeo, mahjongg set in hand, left in a huff.

Something's happened, after all. Why would they suddenly stop coming? Then it hit her like a bolt of lightning. What if they had figured out that she knew! Hamazaki, Kawai, Muraoka—all of them were in on it together. But how could they possibly know? She was imagining things. More likely they just felt like moving their game elsewhere.

On the following day, an inadvertent remark from Shigeo put an end to such wishful thinking.

"Mr. Kawai was really curious about you when he heard that your name was Tomoko. He asked me if you had worked as a telephone operator for a newspaper. He seemed quite interested when I told him you had. He had remembered the articles about your hearing the voice of the midnight murderer. 'So your wife was that operator,' he said. He seemed fascinated. To think that he could remember your name from the newspaper."

Tomoko turned white.

7

Four or five days passed.

In those few days Tomoko started losing weight. She was beset by suspicion and fear. She couldn't tell her husband anything; at this point, it was no longer possible. He seemed to be hiding something, and this prevented her from confiding in him. She was forced to live alone with her secret. And not being able to tell anyone about it was gnawing away at her constantly.

Then she had a brainwave. She needed to talk about it to someone, but it couldn't be just anybody. She had come up with the perfect confidant.

"I'll tell Mr. Ishikawa."

At that time he had been assistant chief of the city desk, and he was the one who had asked Tomoko to make the phone call to get an interview after the death of the scholar. That's how she came to hear the murderer's voice, so in a way Ishikawa was involved. She was trying to justify herself, but there was no one else she could turn to. Two years had passed, and she had no idea whether Ishikawa would still be there or not. Anyway, she would give it a try.

When she went to her old work place she was filled with nostalgia. But when she asked at the main reception desk, she learned that Ishikawa had been transferred.

"Transferred?"

"To the Kyushu branch."

Kyushu. That's so far away, Tomoko thought dispiritedly, her one precious hope dashed. Once more she was all alone.

She went to a nearby coffee shop and ordered a cup of coffee. She had always come here in the past. Now there wasn't one waiter whose face she recognized. Everything was different, everything had been transformed, abandoning her in the process.

In this changing world, how cruel of fate to let that voice pursue me now, she reflected. She was drinking coffee and thinking distractedly when she was suddenly assailed by a doubt. Wait a minute. Was Hamazaki's voice really the same voice? She had convinced herself that it was. But once she began to question it, she started to lose confidence.

When she had worked as an operator, she had trusted her sense of hearing, and everyone used to praise her good ear. But that was two years ago, and two years away from the job gave her doubts.

If I could only hear Hamazaki's voice on the phone one more time, she thought. Then, I'd know for sure whether the voice was the same or not. I've got to hear it once more. There must be some way for me to hear his voice again!

129

On her way home, Tomoko's head was filled with such thoughts. Her husband wasn't back yet. She felt tired. She was sitting in a daze when the woman who ran the neighborhood grocery store called out from the front.

"Mrs. Kotani, are you home?" Tomoko hurried to the door.

"You have a phone call. He wouldn't give his name but said you'd know who he was. He's already called several times trying to get hold of you." The woman was frowning.

Tomoko apologized for causing trouble and rushed out after her. It might be Kawai. He was the one who flashed in her mind first. If it was Kawai, Hamazaki would be with him. She just might be able to hear his voice.

"Hello."

She put the receiver to her ear.

"Mrs. Kotani." It was unmistakably Kawai's high-pitched voice. "Please come right away. Your husband's been taken ill. It's nothing to worry about, but it may be his appendix. Can you come?"

"Yes, of course. Where are you?"

"I'm at 280 Tanimachi in Bunkyo Ward. Change to the streetcar line at Kagomachi and get off at Sasugaya Station. I'll meet you there."

"Oh, by the way, is Mr. Hamazaki there?"

With her husband sick, what could she be thinking of? This was hardly the time to worry about such things. Tomoko was shocked at the way her mind was working. Then again, this might be even more important than her husband's sudden illness.

"Hamazaki?" Kawai's voice hesitated momentarily. "He's not here. Please come right away." There was a hint of laughter in his voice, but Tomoko didn't catch its significance.

"I'll be there. I'm leaving right now."

She hung up and took a deep breath.

She would go and confirm it. One way or another, she had to verify Hamazaki's voice.

PART 2
The Coal Dust

1

Tanashi in Kitatama County is a suburb on the western outskirts of Tokyo, forty-five minutes from Takadanobaba on the Seibu Line. Since it's located some distance from the main railway lines, it has the feel of a rural town; however, with the recent encroachment of Tokyo's population, farmland is gradually being replaced by new housing developments.

In this area traces of the old Musashi plains are still evident. On one side of the tilled fields are groves of various kinds of oak, red pine, and so on. These Musashi woods give an impression of delicacy rather than wildness. "In Japanese literary aesthetics, it is pine forests that have been the focus of attention; one would be hard pressed to find poems in which one listens to the autumn rain from the depths of an oak forest," wrote the late nineteenth-century novelist Kunikida Doppo, who was the first to recognize the special qualities of the Musashi forests.

On that morning—to be exact, around 6:30 A.M. on October 13—a newspaper delivery boy was peddling his bike down a small road from Tanashi to Yanagikubo when his attention was suddenly caught by something beside the road. The leaves on the trees and grass were yellow, but what had attracted the boy's gaze was something lying among the weeds with what looked like a floral pattern on it.

He stopped his bike and approached the thicket. A light gray dress with dark red checks lay in the grass. In the morning air, the colors seemed strangely cold and fresh. When the boy noticed black hair and two white legs sticking out, he jumped on his bike and rushed off in a panic.

One hour later a pathology team from the police department arrived. The three black and white patrol cars were imposing; but there wasn't a soul passing on the quiet Musashi road, just a few people staring from a distance. Residential houses had recently been built here and there in the fields next to the farmhouses. It was that kind of neighborhood.

The dead woman was about twenty-seven years old, of slender build and with delicate features. Her face, contorted as if in pain, was powdered with some kind of blackish substance. The bruise on her throat looked like a red birthmark. It was obvious that she had been strangled.

Since her clothing had not been rumpled, and the grass in the area showed no signs of having been trampled on, it could be surmised that she hadn't put up much of a struggle.

She had no handbag, so there were three possibilities: she hadn't brought one; it had disappeared somewhere; or the murderer had taken it. If the victim hadn't brought one, she probably lived close by. For that matter, she did not appear to be particularly dressed up.

To find out if she lived nearby, the police asked some of the local people standing in a wide circle around the spot to look at the victim. They peered nervously at the corpse, but no one was able to identify her.

"I imagine we'll find out her identity soon enough."

Detective Hatanaka from Police Headquarters was speaking to Chief Ishimaru. Hatanaka had been awakened early and was bleary-eyed from lack of sleep. Chief Ishimaru bent down to look at a gold ring set with jade on her left hand.

After the body was taken away to a hospital for an autopsy, Chief Ishimaru remained behind, staring at the scenery.

"The feel of the Musashi plains still lingers on in these parts," he said.

"I think Doppo's monument is around here, too," answered Hatanaka, who looked off at the line of trees as though he had forgotten all about the murder.

"By the way, did it rain early this morning over where you live?" the chief suddenly asked while looking down at the ground.

"No, it didn't."

"I live in Uguisudani. Around dawn I could hear the sound of rain in my dreams, and when I got up and looked the ground was really wet. But you live in . . ."

"Meguro."

"So it didn't rain over there. Then it was just a passing shower. It doesn't seem to have rained here either." The chief tapped the dry earth with the tip of his shoe.

The results of the autopsy arrived that afternoon. The victim was aged twenty-seven or twenty-eight. Death was due to strangulation. Fourteen or fifteen hours were thought to have elapsed since the time of death, so the murder must have been committed between ten and midnight of the previous evening. There were no external wounds or evidence of violence. The autopsy revealed no traces of poison in the stomach. The lungs were coated with coal dust.

"Coal dust?" Hatanaka asked, looking up at the chief. "I wonder if she lived in a place where there was coal around."

"Hmm."

"The membranes of her nostrils were also coated with coal dust," the pathologist explained.

2

The victim was identified that evening, after the incident had appeared in the newspapers. A man claiming to be her husband contacted the police. He was immediately shown the body.

"Yes, it's my wife," he confirmed.

In response to their questions, he replied that his name was

Shigeo Kotani, thirty-one years of age, of 2-164 Hinode-cho, Toshima Ward, and he was a company employee. He was good-looking, slender, with a fair complexion, and was dressed in the latest fashion.

"My wife's name was Tomoko. She was twenty-eight."

"When did your wife disappear?"

"She wasn't at home when I got back around six o'clock yesterday evening. At first I thought she had gone shopping, but when she still hadn't come back after an hour, I started asking in the neighborhood. I found out that she had been seen leaving the house at around four o'clock."

The lady who ran the grocery store five or six doors down had heard Shigeo asking after his wife, and had gone up to him of her own accord.

"Mr. Kotani, your wife got a phone call at about four o'clock and left in a hurry."

"A phone call?" Shigeo repeated, surprised. "Who was it from?"

"I answered the phone, but he wouldn't give his name. He said your wife would know who he was. She spoke to him on the phone for a bit and then went home. I saw her hurrying off soon after."

Shigeo hadn't a clue as to who could have called. "What did she say on the phone."

"I was busy in the store, so I didn't hear much. She said something about taking the tram to Sasugaya."

Taking the tram to Sasugaya? Everything was making even less sense. Neither of them had anything to do with that part of Tokyo. Shigeo went home and searched for a note, but there was none. Who on earth could have called Tomoko out? It must have been someone she was on close terms with if he had asked for her without giving his name. Was his wife keeping something from him?

Shigeo worried over this the whole night. With his wife still missing, he spent all of the next day at home, fretting. In the evening he saw the newspaper article. He knew it was his wife from the age given and the description of her clothing.

"I bought this jade ring for her several years ago," Shigeo said, pointing to the ring on her lifeless finger.

The police were extremely interested in the phone call.

"Do you have any idea who might have called your wife? Think carefully."

"I've thought about it a great deal, but I can't come up with anyone."

"Had your wife ever gotten other calls like this?"

"Never."

"The body was discovered around Tanashi. Do you have any connection with this area?"

"None whatsoever. It's a mystery to me why my wife would go there."

"Your wife would naturally have taken her handbag when she left the house, but we couldn't find any bag at the murder site. She didn't leave it at home by any chance?"

"No, she must have had it with her. It was a black, square deerskin bag with a golden clasp."

"About how much cash did she have?"

"Hmm, I'd say less than a thousand yen."

"Can you think of anyone who holds a grudge against your wife?"

"No one. I can say that with absolute certainty."

"Do you use coal in your house?" asked Hatanaka.

"No. We use gas, and for baths we go to the public bath."

"Is there a coal-seller in the neighborhood?"

"No."

At this point the police were through with their questions, so after they noted down Shigeo's work address and other particulars, the session ended.

The obvious focus of the investigation was on the mysterious phone call that had lured the victim away. The investigating team called in the woman from the grocery store who had answered the phone. Her story tallied with Shigeo's answers. Hatanaka pressed her a bit further.

"Was it Mrs. Kotani who brought up the idea of going to Sasugaya Station?"

"No, it was more like—'so I should go to Sasugaya Station, then,' as if confirming what the other party had said."

"Did you hear anything else?"

"The store is busy at around four," she answered. "I just happened to overhear that sentence."

"Had there been any such calls before?"

"Let me think." The woman stroked her double chin. "Now that you mention it, there was one."

"Really?" The policemen leaned forward.

"Yes, but it wasn't for the Missus. He wanted to speak to her husband. She came in his place."

"Did he tell you his name?"

"That time, yes. It was, uh, Hama something or other. I can't remember clearly now but I'm sure his name began with Hama."

3

After questioning Shigeo again, the detectives learned about the phone call. One of the detectives summed up.

"It was from a man called Yoshio Hamazaki who works at Kotani's company. That day he was to play mahjongg at Kotani's house; he phoned to say that something had come up and he wouldn't be able to make it."

"Mahjongg, you say? Did you get the names of all the players?"

On a piece of paper stuck in his notebook were written the names Koichi Kawai, Akiharu Muraoka, and Yoshio Hamazaki.

They all worked at Kotani's company and often gathered at Kotani's house for mahjongg; but lately they had been too busy at work to play. Tomoko had not known them well. For her, they were just guests who came to the house for mahjongg. Not one of them was intimate enough with her to invite her out over the phone. Such an idea was inconceivable. And there was no way Tomoko would have accepted such an invitation without telling her husband.

"That's what Kotani said." The detective finished his report.

"What kind of company is it?" Chief Ishimaru asked Hatanaka.

"It deals in medical supplies. Basically, they're middlemen who sell the products of small pharmaceutical companies to whole-salers. It hardly merits being called a company."

The chief thought for a moment. "There might be something here. We should check up on these three—Kawai, Muraoka, and Hamazaki. I want you to find out what alibis they have for last night."

Hatanaka nodded and immediately relayed the order to his men. He looked up at the chief as he sipped his tea.

"If what Kotani says is true, then it's hard to believe one of these fellows called up his wife. What do you think?"

"Kotani seems to be telling the truth. But that doesn't mean one of them didn't have some reason for making the call. What on earth is at Sasugaya? Does any of them live around there?"

Clearly, by "any of them" the chief was referring to Kawai, Muraoka, and Hamazaki. Later, when a detective brought in a file with their addresses, he pounced on it.

"Kawai lives in Nakano; Muraoka and Hamazaki live in the same apartment house in Shibuya. No one lives near Sasugaya."

On the contrary, they all lived quite a distance away.

"Hatanaka, are you checking the Sasugaya area?"

"We are conducting a thorough search. On the assumption that they had arranged to meet at the streetcar station, we've been looking for eyewitnesses among the conductors and passengers, asking if anyone saw someone resembling her in the neighborhood. And from Sasugaya, we've been combing the en-tire area around Shirayama, Komagome, Maruyama, and To-zakicho."

"Let's go take a look ourselves," said the chief, standing up.

"Hatanaka, where do you think Tomoko was killed?" he asked in the car.

"Where?" Hatanaka turned to look at the chief. "You don't think it was where the body was found?"

"Strangulation is tricky. Since there's no blood, it's hard to be sure of the place of death." The chief spoke in the Kansai dialect of his home town. He lit a cigarette, carefully shielding the flame from the wind blowing in from the window, and continued.

"She might have been killed where the body was discovered, or the body might have been brought from somewhere else. The autopsy revealed that the victim's lungs had coal dust in them. In other words, Tomoko inhaled coal dust before she died. However, where the body was found at Tanashi there are no traces of coal."

"Just because she inhaled coal dust doesn't mean that she did it before she was killed. It could have been hours before or even on the previous day," said Hatanaka, trying to find loopholes in the chief's logic.

"If a woman thinks her face is dirty she washes it immediately. Weren't her nostrils also coated with coal dust? It's an unpleasant sensation. So when she washed her face wouldn't she have used a corner of the towel, or something like that, to clean her nose? What I'm saying is that Tomoko was killed before she had time to wash her face. Which means she inhaled the coal dust just before she died."

"I see. That means she was killed someplace else and her body was brought to Tanashi."

"I can't be certain, but it's a possibility."

"So it's vital that we retrace the movements of the victim."

They were approaching the Sasugaya streetcar stop. They stood for a while as a streetcar approached from Suidobashi, lazily making its way up the slope.

The chief surveyed the area. "Let's go over there." He crossed the tracks to a path beside a small shrine that led up a slope. When they reached the top of the hill, the streets spread out below them.

"There aren't any factories here," said the chief as he gazed around. There wasn't even a smokestack. Waves of tiled roofs glistened dully in the autumn sun.

Hatanaka knew what the chief was doing. He was searching for a place with coal.

4

In two days they learned various pieces of information.

Concerning the victim's movements, the search in the Sasu-gaya area had proved fruitless. The woman who ran the grocery store near Tomoko's home had seen her leave around 4:30, which means she would have arrived at Sasugaya Station between 5:00 and 5:30. Since this was the peak of rush hour, she had probably gone unnoticed among the crowds. The streetcar conductors, too, had been unable to help.

Where had Tomoko been between 5:00 and 5:30 P.M. on the twelfth, when she had arrived at Sasugaya, and 6:30 A.M. on the thirteenth, when her body was discovered in Tanashi? Of course, the body had been discovered accidentally at 6:30, and it was im-possible to ascertain how long it had been left there. Assuming that the autopsy was correct and that she had been killed be-tween 10:00 P.M. and midnight on the twelfth, where did she spend her last six or seven hours? Her movements remained a complete mystery. Starting from the other end, if she had gone to the area where the body had been discovered, then she must have used some means of transportation. They decided to check the stations near Tanashi. The closest stop coming from the direc-tion of Tokyo was Tanashi Station on the Seibu Line that started at Takadanobaba. Otherwise, one could take the Seibu Line from Ikebukuro and get off at Tanashi-cho, or the Chuo Line to Musashi-sakai and transfer to a bus. However, none of the station employees at Tanashi, Tanashi-cho, or Musashi-sakai could recall seeing a woman resembling Tomoko. Yet another possibility was that she had hurried over by taxi, so all the cab companies in the city were questioned; but this also drew a blank.

The possibilities would have been narrowed considerably if Tomoko had been killed in one place and her body brought to Tanashi. Trains and buses were all out of the question. The only method of transportation would be either a private car or a cab, with the driver in on the plot. There was no way to disguise a corpse riding in a cab, so the driver had to be in on the crime. If that was the case, the taxi driver wouldn't be likely to come forth as a witness.

The results of the analysis of the coal dust found in the victim's nostrils and lungs arrived. A laboratory in a university mineralogy department conducted the analysis with a special microscope and discovered a 6.70 reflexibility. This indicated an extremely high degree of carbonization, which meant the coal came either from the Chikuho coal mines in Kita-Kyushu or the Yubari mines in Hokkaido.

Other information emerged.

When the movements of Kawai, Muraoka, and Hamazaki from the evening of the twelfth until the morning of the thirteenth were investigated, it was confirmed that Muraoka had gone drinking at a bar in Shibuya and had stayed over at a friend's house in Gotanda, more or less placing him beyond suspicion. As for Kawai and Hamazaki, they had arrived at the house of Yasu Suzuki in Kodaira at around seven o'clock.

"Did you say Kodaira?" Both Ishimaru and Hatanaka shouted in unison. It was a perfectly understandable reaction. Kodaira was just two kilometers from the western outskirts of Tanashi, where the body had been discovered.

"Just who is this Yasu Suzuki?"

According to the detectives, she was Koichi Kawai's mistress and Kawai would stay with her four or five times a month. Kawai had recently built this small house for her, and their life there was no different from that of a married couple's. They even socialized in the neighborhood.

"Sounds a little fishy." Hatanaka scratched his head and ordered a more thorough investigation of their movements that night. As a result, Kawai, Hamazaki, and a woman over thirty by the name of Yasu Suzuki were called to headquarters for questioning.

A rough summary of their testimonies goes as follows: From 3:00 P.M. on the twelfth, Kawai and Hamazaki went to see a movie in Shinjuku. They left the theater around 6:00 and arrived at Yasu's house in Kodaira before 7:00. (The detectives checked up on these statements but were unable to confirm them. Leaving aside the movie, at seven it was already dark, and in the area around Yasu's house on the outskirts of Kodaira the neighbors close their shutters early. Few people pass along the pitch-dark roads, and no one had seen them.)

Around 7:00 Kawai invited three acquaintances in the neighborhood to a folk music concert in Tachikawa. He wanted to express his gratitude because they had been friendly to Yasu. Hamazaki also came along. The concert ended at 9:30. They returned by taxi and arrived at Yasu's just after 10:00.

Kawai then invited them all for a drink at Yasu's. The neighbors refused, but Kawai was so insistent that they finally agreed. First they all went home while Kawai made preparations, and twenty minutes later Kawai himself came to pick them up. Yasu had cooked up a storm. The five men started drinking, but Hamazaki left for some other engagement at around 11:00. Kawai and the three neighbors continued drinking until around 3:30 A.M.; the men stayed over, while Kawai and Yasu slept in the next room.

Around 7:00 A.M. the three wives dropped by to pick up their husbands. Yasu emerged pulling a quilted jacket over her night kimono.

"Just wait a moment while I wake Koichi up," she had said.

The contingent of wives insisted that it wasn't necessary, but she went and woke Kawai up anyway. He looked sleepy as he thanked them and bowed. (This was confirmed by the three neighbors and their wives.)

5

"Hamazaki left Yasu's at eleven."

Both Chief Ishimaru and Hatanaka had fixed on this point. The estimated time of Tomoko's death was between ten and midnight, and less than two kilometers separated Yasu's house from the area where the body was found.

"Wasn't Hamazaki the one the victim spoke to in the first phone call?" the chief asked Hatanaka.

"That's right. He was the one who couldn't come to play mahjongg. Tomoko had gone to the phone in her husband's place."

"It bothers me that he spoke to Tomoko on the phone, even though it was just once. I want to look into it further."

Yoshio Hamazaki was thirty-three, short, with a flattish face and dull eyes. He had a strangely languorous way of talking, and didn't give the impression of being very bright.

He answered their question as follows: "After drinking a bit at Mr. Kawai's (Yasu's house), I excused myself because I wanted to go to the Shinjuku red light district. There's a woman I like who works at a place called Benten. I took the Chuo Line from Kokubunji, got off at Shinjuku, and arrived at Benten around eleven-forty. Her name's A. I stayed over with her. But A. wasn't being very friendly even though I hadn't been there for a while. So we got into a fight and I stormed out at around five in the morning. I took the train to Sendagaya and then slept for two hours on a park bench. I got back to my Shibuya apartment after eight."

Following up on his statement, a detective went to the brothel called Benten in Shinjuku's red light district and spoke to A. She corroborated his story.

"Hama was the one in a bad mood. He was all worked up for some reason and left while it was still dark," A. said. Later it would be apparent that the detective had forgotten to ask one important question.

It was clear that Hamazaki had left Yasu's house in Kodaira at eleven and had arrived at Benten in Shinjuku forty minutes later. Logistically, there was not enough time for him to go to Tanashi, two kilometers from Kodaira, and kill Tomoko. And since he had been with A. at Benten until five in the morning, it would have been impossible for him to have sneaked off unnoticed.

"In which case his alibi more or less clears him of suspicion," said the chief.

"So it seems," Hatanaka replied noncommittally.

"Anyway, it's obvious that Tomoko was killed by someone she knew. That much is certain." Since she had been called away by phone, it had to be someone she was well acquainted with. Otherwise she would never have followed him meekly from Sasugaya all the way to Tanashi.

"Where in heaven's name was Tomoko murdered?" the chief asked as he chewed on his fingernails.

He's thinking about the coal dust, guessed Hatanaka, who was suddenly struck by an idea.

"Chief, could I check the factory coal yards in the city?"

Ishimaru immediately gave his consent. He couldn't shrug off the fact that coal was found in the nostrils and lungs of the victim; still, it would take an enormous amount of time and energy to search every factory coal yard in Tokyo. Exactly how many factories were there? And could their coal yards really provide a clue that would help solve the murder?

It all seemed rather hopeless, but he wanted to give it a try anyway.

The detectives searched for three days with no concrete results.

Chief Ishimaru felt as if he were gazing up at an insurmountable mountain when he had some completely unexpected good news. The expression "a gift from heaven" sounds old-hat, but that's exactly what the chief felt it was.

A report was received that a lost handbag had been turned in at a police box in Tabata on the morning of the thirteenth. It was a black, square, deerskin bag. Inside was a batik purse with 740 yen, some makeup, and tissue paper. There were no name cards. A fourth-grader on her way to school had picked it up in the coal yard of the Tabata Locomotive Depot and had turned it in. The Tabata policemen hadn't realized it was related to the murder and hadn't filed a report with headquarters. A detective who had been out searching the coal yards learned of it when he stopped in at the police box.

The article was immediately sent for and shown to Shigeo.

"It's my wife's," he confirmed.

"Did your wife have anything to do with the Tabata area?"

"Nothing whatsoever," he said, taken aback.

Chief Ishimaru and Hatanaka went to the Tabata coal yard. The girl who had picked up the handbag had been summoned by the police and was waiting there with her mother.

"Where did you find it?" Hatanaka asked.

"Here," the girl pointed.

To the west of numerous lines used for shunting railroad cars was a gigantic crane; underneath it lay a mountain of coal. The mountain had spread out a bit, and the coal had scattered as far as a wooden fence inside the grounds. Running alongside the fence, close to the road, was a rusty, abandoned track. The girl had spotted the handbag while she was walking down the road. It had fallen between the fence and the abandoned track. Around that area were large heaps of what looked like small pieces of coal.

6

Chief Ishimaru and Hatanaka surveyed their surroundings. The crane was breaking up the mountain of coal and dumping it into freight cars. To the east, the shunting of locomotives continued without pause. Mingled with the noise of train whistles and wheels, one could discern the rumbling of the commuter lines in the distance.

To the west of the abandoned track was a row of warehouses, behind which was a road running parallel to the tracks. A constant stream of trucks was speeding down the road, and the area was alive with the clamor common to such places.

"Chief, it's noisy now, but it must get really quiet late at night."

"I was just thinking the same thing."

The estimated time of death was between 10:00 P.M. and midnight. At that hour the area would be as still as the grave. How did the murderer manage to get Tomoko to go there without a struggle?

Indeed, everything seemed to have been carried off without any signs of resistance: the summons over the telephone, getting her to Sasugaya, bringing her late at night to the coal yard at Tabata. There was no evidence of the victim putting up a fight midway, and she seemed to have been compliant in the extreme. Since the murderer had been able to string her along for six or seven hours, it must have been someone she trusted a great deal.

Keeping his eyes on the ground, the chief started to walk around the spot where the girl had picked up the handbag. He hadn't walked more than ten steps when he stopped.

"Hatanaka, look at this." He pointed.

One section of the coal on the ground that had spilled through the fence looked as if it had been flattened with some object.

"Five days have passed since the murder. Somebody may have changed the way it looked."

The chief's subsequent actions made his meaning clear. He went to the office at the far end of the line of warehouses to the left and opened the door. Three station employees who were making small talk turned around at once. He took out his identification.

"On the morning of the thirteenth, was there anything unusual about the area? For example, traces of a fight?"

The last few words immediately rang a bell with them.

"Now that you mention it—I think it was that morning—when we got to work around eight-thirty, we found the coal and earth in one spot all scattered about," one of them said.

The "one spot" he alluded to was the area the chief had pointed out. The man explained how it had looked then.

"It gave the impression that a couple had been fooling around there. A., who works here, found it offensive, so he swept up the scattered bits of coal and earth with a broom."

We could have been spared his good will, the chief thought, but there was nothing he could do about it now. He'd have to make do with a detailed description from A.

When Ishimaru returned to his car, the girl who had found the handbag and her mother were still standing there. Suddenly remembering something he had wanted to ask, the chief approached the girl and patted her on the head.

"When you picked up the handbag, was it wet?"

The girl raised her eyes a little as she gave it some thought.

"No, it wasn't," she replied confidently.

"Think carefully. Are you sure it wasn't wet?" he asked again.

"When I brought it to the police box, I was carrying it in both arms." She meant that she had been able to hold it that way because it hadn't been wet.

When he got into the car, the chief said to the driver, "Take us to Tanashi by the quickest way possible." The driver thought for a moment before he turned the steering wheel. Ishimaru looked at his wristwatch.

Occasionally the chief would glance at the city scenery flowing by. "So now we know where the murder took place," he said to Hatanaka.

"Is it official?"

Hatanaka was also thinking that the murder must have taken place at Tabata, but when he pressed the matter, the chief took out a bulging envelope from his pocket and showed him the contents. Unknown to anyone, he had collected some of the coal flakes and dust in the envelope.

"This will decide everything." He gave a hint of a smile.

From Komagome they drove through Sugamo, Ikebukuro, and Mejiro, came out on Showa Avenue, and headed west, cutting through the Ogikubo intersection onto Ome Highway. The car had zigzagged from one winding road to another before hitting the wide Ome highway, which runs in a straight line west. From here the car effortlessly picked up speed.

When the chief glanced at the speedometer, the needle had reached the fifty-kilometer mark.

After passing through Tanashi, he ordered the driver to take them to the grove where Tomoko's body had been found. He looked at his watch.

"It took fifty-six minutes from Tabata," he said. "If it was at night, a taxi or motorcycle could go as fast as sixty kilometers or so, which makes it, let's say, forty-five minutes."

He was talking about the time it would have taken to bring Tomoko's body here from the Tabata site of the murder.

The chief and Hatanaka got out of the car, stretched, and together breathed in the crisp air of the Musashi plains.

7

On returning to headquarters, Chief Ishimaru ordered two lines of investigation to be followed.

The first was to find out from the Chuo Weather Station exactly what time it had rained in the Tabata area on the morning of the thirteenth. The other was to have the university mineralogy department conduct a chemical analysis of the coal he had collected in the envelope.

After giving these orders, the chief thought a bit as he smoked a cigarette, then placed a sheet of paper on his desk and started writing something in pencil. Just then Hatanaka walked in, but when he saw the chief writing he hesitated.

"Are you busy now?"

"No, come on in," the chief answered, although he didn't stop writing. Hatanaka sat down in a chair nearby.

"Chief, we haven't talked much about this yet, but what do you think the motive for the murder was?"

"Hmm, what could it be?" Ishimaru's pencil kept moving.

"Robbery's been completely discounted, then?"

"Looks that way."

"Which leaves either some grudge or a sexual relationship. But all our investigations have drawn a blank on that point. Tomoko worked as a telephone operator before she married Kotani, and we've even checked into her life back then. She did not have any other boyfriends. She was quite shy by nature, well liked by everybody. It's hard to imagine anyone hating her enough to want to kill her. What's more, there's no question that the murderer in this case was acquainted with the victim. I'm completely at a loss."

"I feel the same way." The chief looked up for the first time— probably not so much to give his opinion but because he had finished writing.

"Seeing that the motive's unclear, we have no choice but to unravel the case by looking at the facts. Take a glance at this." He handed Hatanaka the sheet he had just written. Hatanaka held it in both hands as he read it. It was a kind of summary.

1. Tomoko Kotani. Around 4:00 P.M. on the twelfth she is called to the phone. She leaves immediately, seemingly for Sasugaya. Fourteen hours are unaccounted for until the body is discovered on the morning of the thirteenth; but the autopsy places the time of death between 10:00 P.M. and mid-

night. Supposing she was killed at the Tabata coal yard, then it would have gone like this. Leaves home around 4:30; arrives at Sasugaya Station around 5:00 (assumption); for five to seven hours, whereabouts unknown; between 10 and midnight, killed at Tabata. The next six hours also unclear, but in that time someone moves the corpse. Corpse discovered in Tanashi at 6:30.

2. Koichi Kawai. From 3:00 to 6:00 P.M. on the twelfth in a Shinjuku movie theater with Yoshio Hamazaki (no third witness). Between 6:00 and 7:00, leaves the theater and goes with Hamazaki to Yasu Suzuki's house in Kodaira (only witness, Yasu). From 7:30 goes to hear folk music at Tachikawa with Hamazaki and three neighbors. Concert ends 9:30. Everyone returns together to Yasu's house in Tanashi and parts at 10:10. Invites the three over (substantiated by three neighbors). In the interval, *for twenty minutes* he's with Hamazaki and Yasu in her house (no other witnesses besides Hamazaki and Yasu). Kawai appears at the homes of all three neighbors to invite them again at 10:30. Returns to Yasu's together with the three around 10:50 (neighbors' evidence). They drink until 3:30 the next morning. Afterwards, the three stay the night. He sleeps in the next room with Yasu (neighbors' evidence). Sleeps until 7:30 A.M. At around 7:30 the three neighbors' wives come to Yasu's.

3. Yoshio Hamazaki. From 3:00 to 6:00 P.M. on the twelfth in a movie theater with Koichi Kawai (no third witness). Thereafter his movements the same as Kawai's. At 11 P.M. leaves Yasu's (witnessed by three neighbors). Boards train. At 11:40 shows up at Benten in Shinjuku. Asks for A. After 5:00 on the morning of the thirteenth, argues with A. and leaves Benten in a huff (A.'s statement). For about two hours, until 8:00 A.M., sleeps on a bench in Gaien Park (no witnesses).

4. Akiharu Muraoka and Shigeo Kotani have solid alibis, so will omit.

"It's a little confusing, isn't it?"

"Not at all." Hatanaka pointed to the underlined part. "What did you mean by underlining 'twenty minutes'?"

"For just twenty minutes, corresponding to the interval during which the victim was killed, both Kawai and Hamazaki have blanks in their alibis. In other words, during that time they were alone with Yasu. Since she's Kawai's mistress her evidence doesn't count."

Of course. There was no refuting what the chief said. From 10:10 (when they parted from the neighbors on returning from Tachikawa) until 10:30 (when he repeated his invitation), Kawai and Hamazaki were out of sight of a third party. These twenty minutes coincided with the time of the victim's death.

"However, we've established that the site of the murder was the coal yard at the Tabata Locomotive Depot. The coal dust in the victim's nostrils and lungs, which she must have inhaled just before her death, in all probability matches the coal at the yard. The results of the analysis should confirm this. In which case, even with a blank of twenty minutes, they couldn't possibly have gone from Kodaira to Tabata. When we tested the trip out in the police car, it took fifty-six minutes from Tabata to Kodaira, right? Even speeding, it would take at least forty minutes. The round trip would make it one hour and twenty minutes. Tack onto that the time it took to kill her. As long as they have proof they were in Kodaira, a blank of twenty minutes means nothing."

There was absolutely no way that even the fastest of cars could get from Kodaira to Tabata and back—roughly ninety kilometers—in twenty minutes.

8

The results came in from the two inquiries.

The chemical analysis by the university revealed that the coal the chief had collected in Tabata was the same type as the coal dust found in the victim. When they asked at the depot, they learned that the coal had come from Kyushu's Chikuho coal mines.

"This confirms that the murder occurred in Tabata."

In spite of the results, the chief looked unhappy.

Hatanaka knew how he felt. With the murder site established at Tabata, both Kawai's and Hamazaki's alibis stood up. As they had realized all too well, an unaccounted twenty minutes was virtually meaningless. Someone else had killed Tomoko and carried her body to Tanashi, leaving behind the handbag she had dropped. There was no other logical possibility.

Next came the reply from the Chuo Weather Station. The predawn downpour in the Tabata area on the thirteenth was from approximately 3:00 until 4:50.

"Hatanaka, that's it." The chief showed him the rain chart. "That's our lead."

"Lead?" Hatanaka was puzzled.

"The girl who found the handbag said that it wasn't wet. The Tabata police confirmed this. Isn't that odd? The girl found the bag at eight o'clock, which means the bag would have been rained on for almost two hours. So how could it not have been wet?"

"The bag must have been dropped by the victim at the time of the murder. So naturally it would have been wet from the rain that fell around three."

"Then why wasn't it?"

"The handbag was left there after the rain let up—in other words, after five o'clock."

"Very good. As inconsistent as it is, it's the only logical explanation."

"But since the victim died between ten and midnight, how could the bag have been dropped there after five? It doesn't make sense."

"I said it was inconsistent. But there's no denying the facts. Which means we've made a mistake in our train of thought."

Where had the mistake been made? Chief Ishimaru didn't have the answer either. It was a fact that Tomoko had been killed between 10:00 and midnight at Tabata. It was a fact that at that time Kawai had been in Yasu's house in Kodaira. It was a fact that Hamazaki had left Yasu's, gotten on a train, and stayed over in Shinjuku's red light district. But it was also a fact that the victim's handbag had been left at the Tabata site after 5:00 A.M.

While these were all "facts," they didn't connect with each other. They were like cogs that had gone haywire and were no longer meshing. Each one of them was at cross-purposes with the others.

"They may be all disconnected, but they have the advantage of being truths. In particular, the key to the whole case may be the fact that the handbag was dropped at Tabata after five, just because it's so bizarre. I really don't know—it's all so muddled."

Just then one of the junior detectives came to the door.

"May I come in?"

When the chief nodded, the man approached and made his report to both of them.

"We've conducted inquiries on Yasu Suzuki in the neighborhood. She is Kawai's so-called second wife and seems to be supported by him. Kawai gets along with his neighbors and is well thought of. Nothing out of the ordinary happened on the day of the incident. Everything was just as Kawai testified. But—I don't know whether this will be of any use or not . . ."

"What is it?"

"There's quite a distance separating Yasu's home from her neighbors. The entire area is like that. The houses are set about fifty meters apart. At around 7:00 P.M. on that day, Yasu borrowed a paper fan from her neighbor to the east."

"A fan?"

The chief exchanged glances with Hatanaka. It seemed strange to borrow a fan in the middle of October, but there was an explanation.

"It was the kind of fan used in kitchens. Yasu cooks on oil burners, so she doesn't need to use a fan often. That's why she didn't have one. But when she went to return the fan the next day, she said that she had damaged the one she had borrowed, so she had bought a new one to replace it. The neighbor thought it a little strange that the fan she had lent her, which had been new, would have torn. I don't know whether this is related to the incident, but I thought I would let you know anyway."

After the detective left, Chief Ishimaru and Hatanaka exchanged glances again. They, too, were unable to fathom whether the fan had any significance or not.

9

That evening Hatanaka was called into the chief's office.

Ishimaru, seemingly excited about something, started speaking as soon as he saw Hatanaka.

"Hatanaka, I told you the handbag was a lead, didn't I? Something may come of it."

"What do you mean?"

"Take a look at this."

The chief was pointing at the notes he had made, at the column under Hamazaki's name where he had written: "After 5:00 on the morning of the thirteenth, argues with A. and leaves Benten in a huff (A.'s statement)."

"Oh, I see."

The handbag had been left after five, when the rain had let up.

"For the first time two cogs are meshing. At five o'clock," the chief said complacently. "From Shinjuku to Tabata takes about twenty minutes by train. If he left Shinjuku shortly after 5:00, he would have arrived at the Tabata coal yard around 5:30. Then he could have left the handbag and gone home."

"What? It was Hamazaki who left Tomoko's handbag there?"

"It makes the most sense. Let's work it out logically. Didn't Hamazaki say that after he left Benten he slept on a park bench, leaving him with no alibi? To see if this theory holds up or not, I want to have Benten's A. questioned again."

He immediately sent a detective to Shinjuku. His report brought a smile to Chief Ishimaru's face.

"The night Hamazaki stayed over, he carried with him a small package wrapped in newspaper. It was the shape of a lunch box. When A. asked him what it was, Hamazaki wouldn't reply. A. thought it better not to press the matter, so she left it at that."

This was the substance of the detective's report.

"If only the detective who had first questioned A. had gotten this out of her. How could he have forgotten to ask something as important as whether he had brought anything with him or not?" the chief complained. "Call Hamazaki in right away and question him about the package," he ordered Hatanaka.

Hamazaki was brought in by a detective but refused to admit anything under Hatanaka's interrogation.

"I didn't bring any such thing. A.'s making a mistake."

He seemed quite annoyed at having been hauled in on such a matter. Nostrils flaring, he stuck to his story.

"If you don't know, why don't I tell you then? It was Tomoko's handbag, wasn't it?"

In response to this taunt, Hamazaki simply stared at Hatanaka with his pale, lusterless eyes.

"Gimme a break. I got no reason to have her handbag. Are you saying that I stole it somewhere?" he retorted.

Hatanaka ignored this and continued to press him. "Where did you go when you left Benten after five? You went to Tabata, right? You left the handbag in the coal yard, then returned to your apartment, acting as if nothing happened."

"That's ridiculous. Say whatever you like, but I don't know nothing." He looked away, the color draining from his face. His dull eyes became even more lusterless, but he couldn't hide his trembling. Hatanaka took careful note of his expression before sending him out.

"Chief, Hamazaki did leave the handbag there after all. He's playing the innocent, but there's no mistake."

"What have you done?"

"For the time being all we can do is detain him on suspicion of robbery."

The chief nodded his agreement.

"Where did Hamazaki get Tomoko's handbag? Until we've made that clear, we have no evidence to hold him."

"I've no idea where he might have gotten it. He had also been at Yasu's in Kodaira. It was eleven when he left there. And he showed up at Benten at 11:45, which is exactly how long the train ride would take. He had no time to lure Tomoko to Tabata and kill her. It still doesn't fit in with the other facts."

"Why did Hamazaki deliberately go to the site of the murder in Tabata to leave the handbag?"

"I can't say."

"It would have been after Tomoko's body had been brought to Tanashi. And we still don't know who brought the body there. The cogs still don't mesh, do they?"

Chief Ishimaru found it amusing that Hatanaka had used his metaphor.

"After killing her in Tabata, why would the murderer take the body to Kodaira?" asked Hatanaka.

"He must have felt that it would work against him if it was known that the murder took place at Tabata. Doesn't killing someone at one place and then transporting the body to another place indicate the psychology of a criminal trying to conceal the whereabouts of the murder?"

"Then why deliberately go to Tabata later and leave the handbag? Wouldn't that negate his efforts to conceal the scene of the crime?"

Hatanaka's reasoning had inadvertently made Hamazaki an accessory. Chief Ishimaru didn't contradict him. He had also unconsciously reached this conclusion. Without realizing it, they had formed an idea of who the murderer was.

"That's the problem." The chief buried his head in his arms in exasperation.

It was a fact that Tomoko had been killed at the coal yard of the Tabata Locomotive Depot, even disregarding the trick with the handbag. The proof was the coal dust found in her lungs and nostrils.

It was also a fact that at the estimated time of Tomoko's death, Kawai was at Yasu's house in Kodaira. Three neighbors testified to this. True, there were twenty minutes unaccounted for, but it was impossible to make a round trip from Kodaira to Tabata in twenty minutes. And yet, despite this contradiction, Chief Ishimaru and Hatanaka felt that the beady-eyed, flat-faced Kawai was the murderer.

Hatanaka went home exhausted. Not long before he had installed a bath in his house, the realization of a long-held dream. He had bought it with his summer bonus.

When he got back at around ten, his family had already finished bathing.

"Hey, it's a little lukewarm," he said to his wife as he sank into the water.

She fed the bath furnace with coal. The dark room glowed red from the reflections of the flames.

This reminded Hatanaka of the coal dust that had been found in Tomoko's lungs. The coal he had seen at the coal yard. The coal flakes that the chief had collected in an envelope. The chief had opened the envelope to show him.

The water slowly got hotter. Without moving his hands, Hatanaka sank in up to his shoulders, lost in thought. He was trying to catch hold of an idea that was eluding him, something important. And yet he couldn't capture it. For a while his mind went hazy.

"How's the temperature?"

He gave a half-hearted reply to his wife's inquiry, and mechanically began to soap himself. The envelope with coal flakes which the chief had taken out of his pocket was still on his mind. He kept thinking about it absentmindedly.

He suddenly had a flash of inspiration. Coal could be carried even in an envelope.

Hatanaka leaped out of the bath. He couldn't dry himself fast enough.

"Get my clothes."

"You're going out now?"

"I'm going to the chief's."

He got dressed and left. His heart was pounding. From a nearby public phone, he rang up Ishimaru, who answered the call himself.

"Hatanaka?"

"Chief, I've figured it out. I'm on my way over to explain."

The moment he hung up the receiver, he felt a little calmer. According to his watch, it was just after eleven. He hailed a cruising cab.

Chief Ishimaru had turned on the lights in the living room and was waiting for him. His wife brought them coffee.

"What have you figured out?"

Sensing Hatanaka's excitement, Ishimaru leaned forward in his chair.

"The clue was the envelope you filled with coal," Hatanaka began.

"The envelope?"

"That's right. You put some coal dust from the coal yard in an envelope and took it to be analyzed, right? The murderer did the same thing."

"In which case . . ."

"The murderer collected some dust from the Tabata coal yard in a large envelope or some other container and took it with him. Then, just before he killed the victim at some other place, he had her inhale the coal dust. Most likely he took her to a small room and forced her to inhale the dust. That's why he needed a fan—to blow the coal dust into the air. Whether she liked it or not, the victim would have been forced to inhale it."

While he was speaking, the spectacle unfolded before his eyes. The fan working furiously at the tip of Tomoko's nose. The coal dust flying about wildly. Tomoko choking with pain as she inhaled it. Somebody holding her so she couldn't move.

"The fan would have turned black from the coal dust. They were afraid this might be used as evidence later, so they bought a new one."

"Which makes the Tabata coal yard a cover," the chief growled.

"The murderer was calculating in the extreme. He knew an autopsy would be conducted and the coal dust in the lungs would be discovered. Since she had inhaled it herself, no one would think she had been forced to by another party. If a location with this kind of coal could be found, then the police would conclude that the murder had taken place there."

"Then what was the reason for leaving the handbag in Tabata?"

"To have somebody find it and deliver it to the police. In other words, the murderer wanted to make it doubly clear that that was where the murder had occurred. Otherwise, why go to such lengths to fill her lungs with coal?"

"So the murderer was trying to create an alibi?"

"That's right. He wanted to stress how long the round trip from Tabata to Kodaira took. No matter how fast one went, the round trip required eighty to ninety minutes. It would be absolutely impossible to make it any faster. That's why a gap of only twenty minutes in an alibi could hold up."

"Of course—the gap from 10:10 to 10:30, from when Kawai first parted from the neighbors until the time he went to invite them again," the chief recalled mechanically.

"In those twenty minutes he was at Yasu's. That was probably when he killed Tomoko."

"Which means that Tomoko had been taken to Yasu's house."

"Exactly. He must have called Tomoko out to Sasugaya, then taken her from Suidobashi to Kokubunji on the Chuo Line. After Tomoko arrived with Kawai at Yasu's around seven, she must have been guarded. The houses in Yasu's neighborhood are set far apart, so even if she had screamed a bit, no one would have heard her. Kawai had to create an alibi, so he took his neighbors to hear folk music in Tachikawa a little after seven. The concert ended at 9:30, and around 10:10 they parted in front of Yasu's house. It was then that he would have murdered Tomoko, strangling her after she had been made to inhale the coal. Kawai, Hamazaki, and Yasu were in it together. And the site of the murder was Yasu's house, probably either in a shed or a closet. Afterwards, Kawai went over to his neighbors to invite them. That was around 10:30."

"I see." The chief nodded after some thought.

"Then they started drinking with the neighbors, but as Hamazaki had to leave the handbag in Tabata, he left around eleven. Kawai drank with the neighbors until 3:30 that morning."

"Then when did he bring the body to Tanashi?"

"That would have been after everyone went to sleep at 3:30. Kawai and Yasu slept in the room next to where the neighbors were. That was just a cover. After making sure that everyone was in a drunken sleep, they must have taken the body out of the shed or closet and discarded it two kilometers away, in the western part of Tanashi."

"Two kilometers?" The chief looked at Hatanaka. "I take it they went by car?"

"No, that would have left tracks, so he probably carried the corpse on his back. A woman doesn't weigh much, and for someone as strong as Kawai it would have been quite easy. The only worry would have been passing somebody on the way; but in the countryside around there, no one was likely to be out walking between 3:30 and 4:30 A.M. After they discarded the body in the grove, they walked back to Yasu's. My guess is it was just after 5:00. That's why, when the wives came to Yasu's to pick up their husbands, he was able to greet them rubbing his eyes and acting as if he had been peacefully asleep up until then."

"Incredible," the chief exclaimed. "All I could think about was the distance between Tabata and Kodaira. He had me completely taken in. First thing tomorrow morning we'll search Yasu's house."

"I'm sure they've cleaned up all traces of the coal, but if we can find one or two bits of coal in the corners, we'll be able to nail them."

"Incredible," the chief repeated.

"You mean Kawai? He's clever all right."

"I'm talking about you. I meant how incredible of you to see through his plan."

Kawai confessed ten days later. Hatanaka's theory on Tomoko's murder turned out to be correct. The motive, about which the authorities had been completely in the dark, was unexpected.

"Three years ago Hamazaki and I murdered the wife of an executive in Setagaya. She had cried out while we were robbing the place, and we killed her. Just then the telephone rang. That was a real shock. Here it was the middle of the night and we had just killed someone. Luckily, when Hamazaki picked up the phone, it turned out to be a wrong number. If only he had left it at that, but instead the jerk made some joke about it being the crematorium. As he wanted to keep on talking, I cut him off. Just as I feared, it proved to be our ruin. The woman on the line was a telephone operator for a newspaper. Big headlines appeared in the papers saying that she had heard the voice of the murderer. I really gave it to Hamazaki for being so careless. Then, three years later, he committed another blunder. He let his voice be heard by the same operator. What's more, she was the wife of the newest member of our drug gang. What a strange fate linked us all together! As she had a good memory for voices, she figured out right away that Hamazaki's voice was the same one she had heard back then. Once I sensed that she knew, I couldn't let her live. Her strange desire to hear Hamazaki's voice one more time worked in our favor. When I told her that Hamazaki was with her husband in Kodaira, she meekly followed me there. I guess she wanted to make sure it was Hamazaki's voice. As a result, she fell easily into our trap."

The Woman Who Wrote Haiku

1

When the April issue of the haiku magazine *Cattails* was ready for printing, Bakujin Ishimoto, the head of the editorial committee, held the following discussion over tea with fellow members Riko Yamao, Seisa Fujita, and Shizuko Nishioka. Bakujin was a doctor, and such meetings were always held in his house.

"This month, too, there's no haiku from Sachijo Shimura," remarked Riko, the owner of a second-hand bookstore.

"She never sent us one," Bakujin replied as he looked over the proofs.

"That makes it three times in a row. Maybe she's seriously ill." Seisa, who worked at a trading company, turned to face Bakujin as he spoke. He was single and, at twenty-eight, the youngest member of the editorial committee.

"She's supposed to have a stomach ulcer."

"That's hardly serious, is it? These days ulcers are easily treated by an operation."

"At an ordinary hospital, yes. But I wonder if they'd be able to do the operation right away in that kind of place." Bakujin looked doubtful. By "that kind of place" he meant a charity hospital called Aikoen in H. City in the neighboring prefecture. Sachijo

Shimura had been a contributor to *Cattails* since the previous year. Once Bakujin had chosen her haiku for the lead poem in the magazine. With her contributions, above her name, the word "Aikoen" had been printed in small letters, as if it was her address. She was a patient at this charity hospital.

"You mean they can't operate because of their budget?" Riko asked.

"I'm sure they're on a tight budget. But I can't say that has anything to do with whether they'd operate or not. Anyway, she may not be getting adequate treatment."

Bakujin, who headed a thriving hospital, looked at the others, his glasses glinting in the light.

"What a pity," said Shizuko. She was the wife of a section chief in a large company and the mother of two children. She always had an air of not seeming to lack for anything. "Doesn't she have any relatives?"

"I doubt it, judging from the fact that she's in a charity hospital," replied Bakujin, reaching for a cigarette.

"Just how old is she?" asked Riko.

"She sent me a letter once—remember, it was a thank-you note when her haiku was chosen for the lead. She said she was thirty-three."

Shizuko looked as if she was thinking of the difference between her own age and Sachijo's.

"Has she ever been married?"

"I don't know. We never asked about her personal details." Bakujin's eyes narrowed as he looked at Riko.

"But, seriously, I think we should write her another letter. Since she hasn't contributed any haiku three months in a row . . ."

"Another letter?"

"Actually, last month I sent her a get-well card together with a request for a poem. She only paid her membership fees twice, but I thought we could waive them. Out of all our contributors, she is quite exceptional."

"Absolutely," agreed Shizuko. "I've also had my eye on her. That haiku of hers that we used for the lead was especially good."

"Did you get a reply?" asked Seisa.

"Nothing at all. And she's been such an avid contributor up to now. That's why I am worried that her illness may have gotten worse."

Bakujin blew out smoke.

"Dr. Ishimoto," said Seisa, "please write to her. I don't care about her poem—if she's seriously ill, it'd be enough if we could cheer her up."

"I had exactly the same thought."

"I just remembered one of her haiku. It goes:

> *My solitary self*
> *A cocoon rolls off*
> *The palm of my hand.*

She must be all alone in the world."

"A cocoon? How appropriate." Bakujin rested his elbow on the edge of his desk and looked up. The other three seemed lost in thought.

About a month later the four people gathered once again at Bakujin's home to edit the May issue.

"There's nothing from her this time either," Seisa said to the doctor.

"What? Oh, you mean Sachijo Shimura?"

"I've gone carefully through all the poems, but she hasn't sent anything."

"I wrote to her but received no reply. She didn't have to write one herself—somebody could have helped her with it." Bakujin looked a bit put out.

"What could have happened?" muttered Shizuko.

"You don't think she's dead, do you?" Riko leaned toward Bakujin.

"In that case the hospital would have notified us. Or at the very least it would have returned my letter."

"Maybe the hospital just didn't bother."

"Hmm." Bakujin's eyes seemed to be saying that this was a possibility.

"I can't believe that she's passed away. No matter how bad the

hospital may be, it would surely have sent us some sort of notification. Why, we wrote Sachijo a personal letter. And we've been
sending her our magazine every month," added Shizuko.

"I agree," said Seisa. "She must be critically ill, so bad that
even if someone read the letter to her, she didn't have the
strength to dictate a reply."

"You may be right." Bakujin seemed to have reconsidered.
"Why don't I make inquiries with the doctor in charge at
Aikoen."

"Doctor Ishimoto," said Seisa, "at the beginning of next
month there's the haiku meeting for the A. branch of our association. You're planning on attending, right? A. is near H. City—it's
probably about forty minutes by train. Either before or after the
meeting, do you think you could visit the hospital? If you could
visit her personally, she'd be overjoyed by the honor. It's a Sunday, so I could come with you."

"You seem awfully eager." Bakujin looked at Seisa, and his
eyes behind his glasses crinkled as he gave a light laugh. He liked
to smoke, and when he laughed you could see his stained teeth.
"But it's a good idea—A. *is* close by. If you'll come with me,
Seisa, I don't mind the extra trip."

"Please do try and go," Shizuko urged. "If she has no relations,
I feel terribly sorry for her."

Riko said that he'd like to go, too, provided he could take the
time off. In this way, their plans were finalized.

2

On a clear Sunday in May, Bakujin and Seisa attended the haiku
meeting for *Cattails'* A. branch. Although it was located in
Tokyo, it was very near the neighboring prefecture. Riko had to
attend a second-hand book fair and wasn't able to come.

The meeting ended at three. The branch members invited
them to stay longer, but Bakujin excused himself, saying that he
had some other business, and he and Seisa left on a train for H.
City. Aikoen was located six kilometers from the station, and the
bus ride took them through fields of wheat and rape blossoms,

beyond which lay a large tract of glistening marshland. There must have been a river nearby.

The hospital was in the middle of a wood. At first sight, the three connecting wards—old, decaying structures—seemed gloomy, but a profusion of azaleas was blooming in the flowerbed by the entrance.

At the dusty reception desk a nurse popped her head up and slid open the small glass window.

"We'd like to see Miss Shimura. Sachijo Shimura," said Seisa.

"Sachijo Shimura?" On the other side of the window the gaunt-looking nurse seemed dubious. "Oh, she's been discharged." And she stared at the two.

"Discharged? When?"

"Let me see. About three months ago."

Bakujin and Seisa exchanged glances.

"Then she's better?"

"Hmm." The nurse's expression was vague.

"Do you know her present address, where she went after she was discharged?"

"Hmm."

Bakujin took over from Seisa. He handed the nurse his name card.

"If the director of the hospital is in, I would like to see him about Miss Shimura."

The nurse looked at his card. Along with his name were his medical credentials.

"Wait a moment." The weasely face disappeared. In the time it took her to return and lead them into a bare reception room, they could have easily smoked a cigarette.

The director was a fat man in his fifties with a bright face that contrasted with his surroundings. He was holding a medical chart in his hand.

"So sorry to inconvenience you. I was hoping to meet Miss Shimura, but I was told that she's been discharged," said Bakujin.

"That's right. She left on February tenth." The director glanced at the chart.

"Did she recover from her illness?"

"Have a look at this."

He held out the chart. Bakujin took off his glasses and read it carefully.

"I see." After a while Bakujin raised his head and put on his glasses. "I take it she herself didn't know anything of this?"

"That's correct. We told her she had a stomach ulcer," replied the director.

Then Bakujin and the director talked for a few minutes, their conversation interspersed with German medical terms. Seisa had trouble following the gist.

"Thank you very much," said Bakujin. "I'm not personally acquainted with Miss Shimura, but she frequently sent in contributions for my haiku magazine, and I wanted to visit her."

"Now that you mention it, Miss Shimura always kept a haiku magazine by her bedside," said the director.

"She was an enthusiastic contributor. But for three months straight we heard nothing from her and wondered what had happened," said Bakujin.

"It's been exactly three months since Miss Shimura was discharged."

"But in her condition, what was she planning to do? Did somebody take her in?"

"Yes," the director nodded. "Someone appeared who was going to marry her."

"Marry her?" Both Bakujin and Seisa gave the director a startled look.

"It was all very sudden. Let me explain."

The director smiled and told the following story.

Sachijo Shimura's real name was Sachiko Shimura, Sachijo being a pen name. She had no family. Her legal residence was in M. City, Shikoku, where she was born. Toward the end of the previous year, Aikoen made its regular annual appeal for donations to help its needy patients, and as usual it was written up in the papers. A man named Eitaro Iwamoto from Nakano, Tokyo, sent in 5,000 yen along with a letter saying that as he was from M. City in Shikoku, he'd like the money to go to patients from his home town, if there were any. As Sachijo Shimura was the only patient who qualified, the 5,000 yen was handed to her. Iwamoto was notified, and Sachijo also sent him a thank-you note.

In return, a get-well letter came from Iwamoto, to which Sachijo replied. This correspondence continued for three or four exchanges, until one day Iwamoto came to visit her. He was around thirty-five years of age, and was smartly dressed. At that time, he also gave Sachijo a gift of 3,000 yen. He left after doing his best to cheer up this unfortunate patient from his home town.

Iwamoto returned for two further visits. Who can predict how fate brings people together? At the end of January, Iwamoto told the director that he was going to marry Sachijo and asked for her to be discharged into his care. He explained that he would nurse her back to health himself.

"I have no objection, but do you realize the true nature of Miss Shimura's illness?" the director had asked. "We've told her that she has a stomach ulcer, but the truth of the matter is she has stomach cancer. Even if you marry her, she probably won't live more than four months."

Iwamoto seemed deeply shocked. But after some serious thought, he came to a decision. "If that's the case, it'd be even more of a pity to let her die in such a place. Even if it's just for three or six months, I want to make her last days happy. I want her to die in my home." He then solemnly repeated his request for her to be discharged into his care. The director said that he had been moved by this plea and had given his consent.

"I see. Someone like that came along and Miss Shimura found happiness at last, albeit short-lived," Bakujin commented. "Do you know Mr. Iwamoto's address?"

"Yes. I wrote it down."

The director called in a nurse. This time a young nurse appeared bringing the notebook the director had requested. He flipped through the pages, going down the list of names with his index finger.

"It's in Nakano in Tokyo."

Bakujin jotted down the address in his notebook. "By the way, recently we sent Miss Shimura two letters care of this hospital. Were they forwarded to this address?" he inquired.

The director asked the nurse , and she confirmed that the letters had been placed in forwarding envelopes and mailed.

"I've expressly instructed that mail for discharged patients be forwarded," the director emphasized.

"How odd that there's been no reply." Bakujin looked doubtful. "Maybe the worst has happened?"

"I really can't say. Judging from her condition when she left the hospital in February, four months would have been on the long side."

Bakujin silently smoked a cigarette. Seisa also looked solemn. The light came on above them.

By the time they left the hospital, a pale evening mist had crept up over the surrounding wheat fields.

"Do you think that Sachijo is dead?" Seisa asked Bakujin as they waited on the country road for the bus.

"She may be. According to her medical chart, there was no mistaking the symptoms. And the cancer was already quite advanced." Bakujin's stoop made his stocky frame appear even shorter. "Today's May tenth. She was released on February tenth, so it's been exactly three months. It's a definite possibility."

"If it's true, I feel so sorry for her," said Seisa haltingly.

"We should be thankful that such a compassionate man came along. Quite something, wasn't it? Think of all the patients who die alone. One way of looking at it is that Sachijo found true happiness. Poised on the threshold of death, she was able to experience love."

The two returned to Tokyo late that evening.

3

The next morning Seisa dropped by while Bakujin was still in bed.

"You're awfully early, aren't you?"

"I'm on my way to work. Last night I went through the old issues, rereading Sachijo's haiku." Seisa's youthful eyes were shining. "She was in love after all. This is one of the last poems she wrote:

Waiting for spring
Waiting for him to come
I brush the edge of my quilt.

On her dreary hospital bed, she was waiting for Iwamoto."
"I see." Bakujin rubbed his eyes sleepily. "Sachijo found happiness at last, then?"
"Dr. Ishimoto," Seisa leaned forward, "I want to find out what's happened to her. If she's dead, I'd like to offer incense at her household altar. You wrote down her address, didn't you? Please give it to me and I'll drop by on my way home from work."
Bakujin stood up, got his notebook from his pocket, and took off his glasses.
"Here it is."
Seisa copied the address down in his own notebook. Bakujin lit a cigarette as he watched him.
"Since yesterday you've been awfully anxious about Sachijo."
"We're the ones who liked her haiku enough to choose them. I feel close to her somehow," said Seisa as he handed the book back.
Bakujin quickly nodded in agreement. "Her haiku was selected for our lead poem, so of course she's important to us. Go and see how she's doing."
Seisa bowed and left. Bakujin went to wash.

All that day Bakujin was busy with his hospital duties. When Seisa returned around eight, the doctor was enjoying a nightcap. Seisa looked depressed.
"Did you go?"
"Yes, I did."
"You must be tired. Have a drink." Bakujin poured him a drink, but Seisa left it on the table. "Well, how is she?"
"She died." Seisa spoke in a hushed tone.

"I thought so from the moment I saw your face. What a shame," Bakujin sympathized. "Did you manage to offer some incense?"

"Her husband's moved away. It's been a month already." Seisa reached for his drink.

"Moved? Then how did you find out about her death?"

"I heard it from the neighbors. This is what happened," Seisa recounted.

It was around six o'clock when Seisa, on his way home from work, arrived at the Nakano address. The house in question, about a twenty-minute walk from the station, had been extremely difficult to locate. It was an old, smallish house tucked away in the middle of a residential district. But when he rang the bell, the person who came to the door told him that he had only recently rented the place and that the previous tenant—Mr. Iwamoto—had moved out about a month earlier, shortly after the death of his wife.

Seisa then went to see the landlord, who filled him in on the details. Iwamoto had rented the house around November of the previous year. He was single and worked for a company in the Marunouchi district. He was away as much as twenty days a month on business trips, and the house was usually locked up. The neighbors often gossiped about the extravagance of paying so much rent. When they looked over the fence, they occasionally saw Iwamoto cleaning the house.

Around February, however, his wife came to live with him. She never left the house as she was sick and bedridden. Twice a week a doctor, not someone known in the area, would make a house call. As before, the husband was away frequently. Perhaps because he couldn't take care of his wife himself, he hired a housekeeper. She did not go out often either. As is normal in Tokyo, the Iwamotos did not socialize with their neighbors, so no one really knew very much about them.

Around the beginning of April, the neighbors heard an automobile pull up in front of Iwamoto's house several times in the middle of the night. The next day there was an "In Mourning" notice posted on the door. It was then that the neighbors learned that his wife had died. That afternoon a hearse came for the body. Iwamoto didn't seem to have any friends or relatives, for he was alone as he rode in the hearse to the crematorium. His neighbors, who were the only ones to see him off, remarked that they had never witnessed such a wretched, lonely funeral. Three days later, two or three people who seemed to be relations arrived.

Perhaps Iwamoto was embarrassed by the funeral, or it could be that after losing his wife he no longer wanted to remain in the same house. In any case, before long he gave notice to the landlord and moved away.

"The landlord told me that his heart went out to Mr. Iwamoto. Sachijo died only two months after he had married her." Seisa spoke somberly.

"Just as I had feared," Bakujin muttered.

"Is stomach cancer really so relentless?"

"Cancer can be quick. In February, when the director of Aikoen told Mr. Iwamoto that she had about four months left, he was speaking in terms of the maximum period. She ended up living only two more months. What a terrible shame. Sachijo's happiness did not last very long, did it? In the editor's column for the next issue I'll include an obituary."

"I feel sorry for this Iwamoto, too."

Seisa was a bit drunk when he left a little after ten. Bakujin went to take a bath.

While soaking in the tub, Sachijo's death and her short-lived happiness continued to prey on his mind. It had been a lonely funeral, but Iwamoto's solitary farewell was surely all she could have wanted.

While he was ruminating on this, he suddenly stared up at the steam-shrouded ceiling. He had had an idea. For a while he remained lost in thought.

4

The next day Bakujin telephoned Seisa at work and asked him to drop by that evening.

Seisa arrived around seven o'clock.

"What did you want to see me about?"

"It's about Sachijo Shimura."

"I see her death has been bothering you as well. Somehow I was out of sorts all last night." Seisa rubbed his cheek.

"There's something I wanted to ask you. According to the landlord, three days after Sachijo's funeral, some people who seemed to be relatives came to see Mr. Iwamoto. Is that right?"

"Yes."

"Sachijo had no relatives, so they must have been Mr. Iwamoto's. But wasn't it a bit late for them to come, three days after the funeral?"

"But if they live in his home town in Shikoku, that's how long it might have taken them to get to Tokyo."

"Of course—Iwamoto came from Shikoku. In that case, it stands to reason. Still, as Sachijo and Iwamoto had been living together for only two months, they probably hadn't formally recorded their marriage in the family register. Mr. Iwamoto's relatives would have been informed by letter, but they had probably never met her, so they can't have been very close. So would they really go to all the trouble of coming to Tokyo because of her death?"

"I see what you mean. All the same, Sachijo was Iwamoto's wife, even if only for two months. When his relations received a telegram informing them of her death, they might very well have decided to come to Tokyo. Country folk have a strong sense of family obligations."

"I wonder." Bakujin thought as he smoked a cigarette. "By the way, didn't you say that the night Sachijo died an automobile was heard at the house several times?"

"Yes."

"I'd like to have more details, such as when and how often. This time talk to the neighbors rather than the landlord. They might know more. I also want you to find out if Mr. Iwamoto can drive."

"What's this about? Do you have doubts about the cause of Sachijo's death?" Seisa's eyes widened.

"I'm not especially doubting it. I'd just like to know." Bakujin was vague.

"Well, if you insist, I'll do as you ask."

"Now don't get offended. Oh, there's something else important. Who was the doctor who made the house calls on Sachijo? You said that he isn't known in the area, but find out if there's anyone in the neighborhood who recognized him. Also . . ."

"Let me write this down." Seisa reached into his pocket for his notebook. He used this same notebook for the haiku he composed.

Bakujin continued. "Next, I want you to find out the funeral parlor that handled the arrangements. And this is the most important item. After Sachijo came to live with Iwamoto, you said that a housekeeper was employed. Try to find out which agency sent her."

"That's everything? Right, I've got it."

Seisa looked as if he wanted to ask something but stopped, and he left soon after.

He returned two days later, in the evening.

"Sorry to have taken so long."

"Not at all. I appreciate your hard work. So what did you find out?" Bakujin leaned forward.

"Not very much." Seisa looked discouraged as he gave his report. "I asked the next-door neighbors. Since they hadn't got to know Iwamoto well, they couldn't tell me much. But the night Sachijo died, their son, who's going to college, had been up late studying and he heard the automobile."

Seisa was looking at his notebook as he spoke.

"The first time the car pulled up in front of the house was around eleven o'clock. Then there was the sound of the front door opening and somebody entering; clearly someone had gotten out of the car and gone into the house. He said he heard a woman's voice at the same time."

"Did you say a woman's voice? It must have been the housekeeper then."

"He said it wasn't. He had heard the housekeeper's voice a few times, but this one sounded different. About one hour later, the engine was started and the car went off. He didn't hear any voices that time. He finished studying and was washing before going to bed when he heard a car pull up once again. This was around two in the morning."

"Wait, wait." Bakujin was taking notes with a pencil. "So was the car still in front of the house the next morning?"

"No, it left around six o'clock. The woman next door, who was already awake, heard it leave. And it seems that Iwamoto can drive. He was once seen driving to the house in a Renault or some such fancy car."

"Fine. Let me summarize what you've told me."

Bakujin made up the following list on a fresh sheet of paper.

Automobile (arrived) approx. 11 P.M.
(left) approx. midnight
(arrived) approx. 2 A.M.
(left) approx. 6 A.M.

"Now, how about the doctor?"

"Nobody in the neighborhood knows who he is. He's an elderly man who came about twice a week."

"What about the funeral parlor?"

"Since no one in the neighborhood knew which one it was, I asked at several local ones, but none of them had any record of handling a funeral at that time for a family named Iwamoto."

"I really put you to a lot of work, didn't I? Did you get the name of the housekeeping agency?"

"No luck there either. It seems the housekeeper never spoke to anyone in the neighborhood. I was told that she was around thirty—good-looking and vivacious."

"Hmm, I see." Bakujin, lost in thought, left his cigarette to smolder unattended as he closed his eyes.

"Dr. Ishimoto, is there something fishy about all this?" Seisa sipped his tea and looked at Bakujin.

"I wouldn't say fishy exactly." He opened his eyes and smiled at Seisa. "Anyway, don't worry about it. And thanks for all the trouble you've gone to."

Seisa returned his smile. "Sachijo seems to have got you under her spell, too."

5

The next day Bakujin took care of his hospital duties in the morning and then left.

First he went to the Nakano Ward Office. In answer to his question, a clerk informed him that in April there was no record of a cremation certificate issued under the name of either Sachiko Shimura or Sachiko Iwamoto. He then made inquiries at four or five funeral parlors in Nakano Ward but drew a blank.

Next Bakujin went to the Medical Association's office to put in a request for an inquiry. Two days later he had the results. The doctor who had made house calls at the Iwamoto address and who had signed the death certificate was a physician from Ikebukuro by the name of Y.

Bakujin telephoned Y.

"Was the name of the patient at that address Sachiko Iwamoto or Sachiko Shimura?" he asked.

Y. had the file brought to him.

"No, her name was Yasuko Kusakabe, aged thirty-seven, wife of Shunsuke Kusakabe."

Yasuko Kusakabe, wife of Shunsuke. Bakujin jotted down the names. His fingers gripping the pencil trembled in excitement. "Wasn't that the Iwamoto residence?"

"Yes, it was. The name on the door was Iwamoto. I thought it a little strange, but when I asked Mr. Kusakabe, he told me that he was sharing a friend's house," the doctor answered.

"I see. And the patient's illness?"

"She had cancer of the stomach. When I made my first house call, the case was already hopeless. But I kept going for a month. I had never worked in Nakano before—it was the first time I had been called out to the area. That struck me as somewhat unusual."

"What was the time of death?"

"I was told over the phone that she had died so I went immediately and arrived at 11:30 P.M. on April tenth. According to her husband, she had died about an hour earlier. The condition of the body more or less matched with this time, so that's what I wrote on the death certificate."

"When you came was anyone else there?"

"Just her husband and a woman who seemed to be the housekeeper. They were both crying."

"Thank you very much."

After Bakujin hung up, he stood motionless for a while. Then he sent for his car and headed for the police station.

One week later a thirty-eight-year-old man called Shunsuke Kusakabe was arrested in Shinagawa on suspicion of murdering his wife. He was living with his mistress, the woman who had pretended to be his housekeeper.

Shunsuke's motive was to free himself of his wife and collect on her two-million-yen life insurance policy. His mistress had a friend who was a nurse at Aikoen and had heard from her of a charity patient named Sachiko Shimura who was alone in the world and approaching death. When she mentioned this to Shunsuke, he came up with the following plan. He'd take Sachiko to live with him, and when she died he'd have the death certificate made in his wife's name. They were close in age. His mistress had been told by the Aikoen nurse that Sachiko was born in M. City in Shikoku, so Shunsuke used his contribution to someone from his "home town" as a way to get to know her. He made frequent visits and pretended to be in love with her. The love-starved Sachiko was quick to reciprocate. When he asked her to marry him, she was overjoyed. He brought her to the Nakano house, which he had rented at the time he had conceived his plan.

Sachiko, or Sachijo to use her pen name, didn't know she had cancer. To the very end she believed she had an ulcer; so when Shunsuke asked her to recuperate at his home, his kindness had moved her to tears. He even hired a housekeeper. Sachijo had no inkling that she was really Shunsuke's mistress and an accomplice in the crime.

Shunsuke's real home was in Setagaya, where he lived with his wife. That was the reason he had to leave his Nakano house on frequent "business trips." His plan had been executed with great caution; all he had to do was wait for Sachijo's death.

Sachijo died on April 10, just after 10 P.M. Before she died she seemed to have caught on to the housekeeper's real identity, but there was no longer anything she could do about it. The moment she breathed her last, Shunsuke, who had the good luck to be present, hastily returned to his Setagaya home and brought his wife with him by car. He had borrowed the car from a friend in the neighborhood. He made up some pretext to lure his wife into the Nakano house. As she got out of the car, she said something. This was the voice the neighbor's son had heard.

As soon as she was inside the house, Shunsuke pulled her down from behind and strangled her. His mistress covered her mouth and held her hands down. Once she was dead, they hid the body in the back of the house. Then Shunsuke went to a nearby public phone booth and called the doctor.

The doctor verified Sachijo's death and wrote out the death certificate in the name of Yasuko Kusakabe, just as they had planned.

As soon as the doctor left, Shunsuke put his wife's body in the coffin he had bought and closed the lid. He said that he did not want to wake the neighbors by hammering the lid down in the middle of the night, so he waited until dawn to do this. In the meantime he carried Sachijo's body to the car out front and drove off. This was around midnight; the same boy next door heard the car pull away.

Shunsuke sped down the Koshu Highway and discarded Sachijo's body in the Kitatama area, by the side of a deserted road surrounded by rice fields. He was back about two hours later, and once again the student heard the car returning. For the two hours Shunsuke was away, his mistress waited alone by the side of his wife's coffin.

He couldn't very well leave the car he had borrowed where it was. He had to return it to its owner. So around six in the morning Shunsuke drove the car back. This was what the woman next door heard when she was getting up.

When Shunsuke had discarded Sachijo's body on a country road, he had hoped that it would be taken for that of an unknown vagrant who had died. He had even dressed Sachijo's body in shabby clothes. Later investigations revealed that his scheme had worked and that Sachijo's body had been given a provisional burial by the local authorities.

Shunsuke subsequently informed his wife's relatives in Hokkaido of her death. They came to his Nakano home in Tokyo and prayed before her urn on the household altar. His wife wrote to her relatives only two or three times a year, so they hadn't questioned Shunsuke's move to Nakano.

As for the funeral parlor, both Bakujin and Seisa had drawn blanks because they had made inquiries about the name Iwamoto. A funeral parlor in Nakano—which had a cremation certificate for a Yasuko Kusakabe—had driven the body in a hearse to the crematorium. They told the police that they thought it strange the body was already in the coffin with the lid nailed shut when they got to the house. They had been taken aback by this frightening show of efficiency.

Shunsuke had collected the insurance money, sold his house in Setagaya, and moved with his mistress into an apartment in Shinagawa when he was arrested. After the incident appeared in the papers, Seisa came to see Bakujin.

"What made you suspicious?" he asked.

"First of all, it was the relatives coming three days after the funeral. But even more suspicious were the frequent trips made with the car."

Bakujin took out the memo he had written. The words "arrived" and "left" were each written down twice. Seisa glanced at it.

"But even so, this isn't enough. Look, didn't the doctor say that he came by car around 11:30 to write out the death certificate? Why is there no record of his car coming?"

Bakujin smiled gently at Seisa.

"The roads are narrow in that neighborhood. I went there myself. The doctor's car was too big to pull up in front, so he parked on the main street. The car that Kusakabe borrowed was a small Renault. Wasn't it you who told me that someone in the neighborhood had once seen him pull up to the house in such a car?"

Then Bakujin added, "I'll write a eulogy for Sachijo Shimura in the editor's column."